Donna Rose
and the Slug War

This novel is a work of fiction. Names, characters, places and incidents are either the product of the author's imagination, or, if real, used fictitiously.

First Edition
First Printing: August 2004

Published in 2004 in conjunction with Tekno Books and Ed Gorman.

Set in 11 pt. Plantin by Christina S. Huff.

Printed in the United States on permanent paper.

Library of Congress Cataloging-in-Publication Data

Johnson, Norma Tadlock.
  Donna Rose and the slug war / Norma Tadlock Johnson.
  —1st ed.
      p. cm.
    ISBN 1-59414-220-3 (hc : alk. paper)
    1. Women detectives—Washington (State)—Fiction.
  2. Washington (State)—Fiction.   3. Retired teachers—Fiction.
  I. Title.
  PS3560.O3819D66 2004
  813'.54—dc22   2004046969

Donna Rose and the Slug War

Norma Tadlock Johnson

Five Star • Waterville, Maine

For my beloved family,
Karl, Grace and Janice Kay Johnson,
Sarah and Katie Baczewski.

CHAPTER I

The early bird catches the worm and also gets the most clams.
Unfortunately, this early bird also found the body.

Police Chief Donniker took his time getting there after I
called from the public phone on the dock, which wasn't surprising. He's not the swiftest, mentally or physically. Never
has been. He wasn't as a kid in my very first classroom of
sixth-graders, when his greatest skill was his aim with spit
wads, and he hasn't improved.

He lumbered out of the patrol car, where the light flashed
unnecessarily on top. Not many people out-and-about
shortly after dawn in Cedar Harbor. Actually, he'd used more
restraint than I'd been expecting when he didn't arrive
blasting his siren.

"Where's the body, Ma'am?" he asked, straight-faced.
He'd been watching too much TV. "Ma'am," indeed.
"Teach" was about as good as I ever got out of him in the
sixth grade.

"Right there—Billy." I swallowed as I pointed to the
blimp-shaped lump lying out on the sand of the tide flats and
visible even from the top of the bank where we stood. I know
only one person with a body like that, but I hadn't gone close
enough to confirm my supposition.

"Don't call me Billy," Chief Donniker snapped.

I shrugged. "I won't if you don't call me Ma'am."

He glared at me, then headed down the stairs to the beach.

7

I turned to follow him, but waited when I heard another car approaching. I was relieved to see that it was driven by young red-haired Jake Santorini, the new man in the police department. Jake has a head on his shoulders, if I'm not mistaken. We exchanged greetings, then hurried down the stairs to join the Chief, who stood over the body, rubbing his chin with his hand.

The earlier pink of the sky was fading, but the morning haze still hung over the gently lapping water. No one else was on the beach yet, if you didn't count the blue heron that gave a squawk of disapproval, then flew ponderously a little farther down the sand. Jake and I watched the Chief and waited for his painfully slow thought processes to come to a conclusion.

"Lyle Corrigan," the Chief finally announced.

"Uh-huh," I said.

"Been murdered," he stated.

"Uh-huh," I said again. This time I thought *I* showed restraint. It doesn't take a genius to determine that drowning victims don't normally have round holes in their foreheads.

I shouldn't have spoken at all. It reminded him of my presence. "Ma . . . I mean, Mrs. Galbreath, this is a police investigation. We'll get in touch with you later."

"Sure," I agreed. I wasn't interested in the mechanics of removing a murder victim. If I had to find a body, I was glad that it was someone I disliked. Made it a little easier to distance myself and maintain control. I managed to wink at Jake as I turned and left, avoiding looking at the body again.

The town was waking up now. Al Parry was heading in the front door of the bakery for his usual coffee and two—or three—doughnuts, which undoubtedly contribute to a soaring cholesterol. He's a pharmacist and ought to know better. Across the street, Al's teenage son, Brad, was sweeping the sidewalk in front of The Drugstore. Just beyond, the windows of Corrigan's Hardware were unlit. Lyle normally would have opened the store by now. As I watched, the young man who worked for him arrived, tried the door, then stepped back to stare at the store with a puzzled expression. Someone would have to tell him.

He was going to find out real soon, along with everyone else. The aide car-ambulance-hearse that serves the dead and nearly dead of Cedar Harbor roared down Main Street just then and parked next to the dock. Heads turned and Al and a couple of his buddies popped out of the bakery to gawk and then to hurry toward the water. Fortunately it wasn't going to be up to me to spread the word.

I felt the strength ebb out of my body, as if someone had pulled the plugs at the ends of my toes. Adrenaline had kept me going. Now I could go home and recuperate.

Lyle's death was still the main topic of conversation at any gathering in Cedar Harbor. If the Chief had made any real progress during the past week in ascertaining the murderer, no one had heard about it. Of course, he couldn't find a killer unless the scoundrel popped up in front of him with a gun in his hand. If that sounds as though I don't have any faith in him, you've got it.

I was working in my garden while I mulled over the unlikelihood of murder in our community. My garden is my therapy. Just walking through it, dead-heading a rose here and there, propping up sagging peonies, makes me feel better when I need it, but working seriously, as I was this time, always helps my brain cells function on a different level. I sat on my kneeling bench thinking while I yanked out pesky chickweed that was hiding under the spreading leaves of perennials.

Murder. Cedar Harbor is so peaceful, beautiful, out of the

mainstream from crime. And yet—anger is here, too, I had to admit. Tuesday's water board meeting was an example. Being on the board is one of the tasks I do still take on. After all, who is more interested in water than a dedicated gardener? Besides, someone has to keep an eye on those idiots who make up the rest of the board.

This time Al Parry was mad at me. *He* had the nerve to suggest that we ban all watering of gardens since we were in the middle of a drought. *I* pointed out that dry spells were a part of the normal cycles of weather in the Pacific Northwest, we had no indication that our water system was in trouble, and besides, I felt that all those with hot tubs should be required to drain them first. I made a motion to that effect.

I thought I was being tactful in not naming names, but Al didn't think so. Everyone knows he has a huge, deluxe model in his backyard that accommodates the entire neighborhood. Except me, of course. I've never been invited. I thought Al was going to explode like the red balloon he resembled by the time he finished yelling. Nobody seconded my motion.

Lyle had been on the water board, too, chairman in fact, so now we were one member short. Anyone the district chose at our annual meeting in August would be an improvement.

My searching fingers touched the slime of a slug, and I jerked my hand back. Yuck! I folded the leaves of the foxglove out of the way and studied the beast. One of the brown ones, but big. Five inches at least. Where had it been that I hadn't found it before? It curled into a ball trying to hide. I hate slugs with a passion, but still they deserve to live like all of God's creatures. I reached for the tongs on the ground beside me, then maneuvered the mucus-covered gastropod into a cut-off milk carton to join its friends. Later I'd dispose of them in Cyrus Bates' vegetable garden. He'd undoubtedly kill them when he found them, but that was his problem and on his conscience, not mine. Anyway, they'd have a few more days of life.

The slug had distracted me. Murder of humans was what I wanted to think about. Specifically, the whys and hows and whos. Most people who knew Lyle have wanted to murder him at one time or another. I'd felt that way myself, even though I have a reverence for life. Lyle—and slugs. There was a resemblance, come to think of it, more than just the juxtaposition in my thoughts. The slug I'd just popped into the container had an unfortunate similarity to his body as it lay, sprawled on the sand. That was one scene I'd prefer to put out of my mind forever. What an unpleasant end for anyone.

"Hi, Donna. I thought I'd see if you were working back here."

I turned, glad for the break. Sue Reilly stood just beyond the gate in my picket fence. She always looks crisp and clean. Her dark hair gleamed in the sun. So nice, in this day when many young people look as if they haven't combed their hair since their mothers stopped doing it for them. "Come on in, if you have time," I called. "My new David Austin rose is blooming. I want to show it to you."

"All the time in the world," she answered, opening the gate and pushing the stroller with her two toddlers inside. That's another nice thing about her. She's careful that those youngsters don't damage anything in my garden. They're normal kids and I wouldn't mind that much, but still, it's good to see a mother who cares. Such a shame that she has to bear the burden of widowhood. The gate swung shut behind her.

"Let them out," I suggested. "They won't do any real harm. How are you today, Todd and Jeff?" They didn't answer, not surprising at two and three, but they grinned with smiles that matched their mother's.

Sue unfastened them and pulled a large rubber ball from the hamper on the back of the stroller. "Here, boys," she said, tossing it to Jeff. "Just be careful of Mrs. Galbreath's flowers." They laughed and began to run and roll on the grass. Nothing like watching children—or puppies—at play to put one in a good humor.

"Just a second," I said, "while I move the hose." I shut off the faucet, then unscrewed the hose that led to my perennial bed soaker. I dragged it over to the shade garden as she said, "That rose *is* lovely, with that creamy yellow color. What's it called?"

"That's Graham Thomas," I answered as I screwed the attachment. I walked back to the house and turned the faucet on. One of these days I was going to have to install a system. Those computerized ones I've seen in catalogs would be nice. A faint hissing and a scattered spray indicated that it was working.

"Gotcha!"

I spun around, startled but not surprised. Cyrus Bates's expression was as triumphant as his words. He had to be standing on a bench as he peered over his high cedar fence— the Berlin Wall, I call it—and pointed to the soaker.

"It's not our day to water, Donna," he said in that infuriatingly patronizing tone he likes to use with me. "You know that. I figured you were cheating. You always do."

Sue stared at him, bewildered.

"Oh, dry up, Cyrus," I said, inwardly pleased at my choice of words. So appropriate for the circumstances. "You know very well that the regulations are unreasonable. How can I possibly do all these beds if I water only every third day and before ten o'clock in the morning?"

"You have the option to do it in the evening."

"Who are you kidding? After nine o'clock? I'm too old for

12

that. Besides, you know as well as I do—you're enough of a gardener for that . . ." His face stiffened, but I went on. "You know everything would mildew if I watered at night. That's all very well for a lawn." I shrugged. "I suppose it wouldn't even hurt your vegetables."

"Of course it would. *I* get up early in the morning on my days and *get it done*." He sounded just like the military man he'd been.

"Well, *I* don't. I didn't tend kiddies all those years at the crack of dawn to get up early now unless I have to." I was thinking of my foray just last week that had resulted in my finding the body. "Don't be sanctimonious, Cyrus. Although, you always are."

He growled, and the tips of his straw-colored moustache that he's so vain about quivered. "The board'll hear from me about this," he said, and then he disappeared.

Sue cracked up and so did I. "Is he always like this?" she asked before her laughter pealed loud and clear.

I hoped Cyrus was listening. I nodded. "Always. You can see what a burden it is to live next door to him."

I heard shrubbery rustling on the other side of the fence. With luck, he'd fallen into his raspberries. Then, with humphs and grumbles, he headed toward his house.

"I don't want you to think I waste water," I said. "I'm really very careful. It's just that, at my age . . ."

"Oh, pooh," Sue said. "Your age, hah! I think you enjoy battling with him."

I contemplated that for a minute. "You know, I do believe you're right. Do you suppose he enjoys it, too?" What a horrid thought. "No," I decided. "Cyrus doesn't enjoy anything."

I studied Sue for a moment. "How would you like to be on the water board?"

"Oh, no, you don't," she said, holding up a hand and backing up.

"Come on," I pleaded. "We need one reasonable, rational voice—besides me, of course."

She shook her head vehemently. "If nothing else, I'd have to get a babysitter every time they met, and I can't afford to. I use my babysitting money to practice with my string quartet."

"That's right," I said morosely. "I forgot. Oh, well, it was worth a try. Anyway, they'd have just wanted you to be secretary. That's the only reason they ever choose a woman."

"How about you? You've never been secretary."

I snorted. "I surprised them. How I enjoy watching Cyrus taking notes. He always forgets to do it half-way through the meeting."

"I've just been down to the post office," Sue said. "Here, Jeff." She picked up the red ball and tossed it to him. He'd just crashed into a Shasta daisy clump, but they're tough and I didn't say anything. Diverting him was the best thing to do. "What a lot of gossip you hear there," she continued.

"Oh?" I waited.

She smiled. "Of course if you're not interested . . ."

"Don't tease. You know I am."

"Well, Mark Gasper's back hanging around town. He was Dale's boss, you know." Her face softened at the mention of her dead husband. It had only been recently that she'd been able to talk about him at all.

"So?"

"Well, everybody was wondering if he's going to be able to pull off that development now that Lyle's dead. Dale and I had such mixed feelings about so many houses being built here, you know that, even if Dale worked for him."

"I don't see," I said, mulling it over, "what Lyle's being

14

gone would have to do with it. Just because he was instrumental in getting the county to declare a moratorium . . ."

"More than instrumental, people are saying. I don't know, but I do know Dale used to wonder. Mark was so good to me, though, after Dale's accident, and—and I hate to think he'd do anything shady."

"Uh-huh." I didn't respond to her comment about the head of Gasper Enterprises. Lots of people thought he was capable of shady behavior, but then not everyone is rational when discussing the pros and cons of development. I'm old enough to see both sides. Of course I'd like Cedar Harbor to stay exactly the same, an enclave of peace in the middle of turbulence, but it's not going to. Any fool should be able to see that. If nothing else, Lyle's murder shows that it's changing.

"What else did you hear?" I asked.

"Nothing important. Have you seen that new woman who moved into the Satterburg cottage? I feel so sorry for her. So fat, and that bleached blond hair . . ."

I nodded. "Yes. I saw her yesterday myself, and had the same thought. I'd like to get my hands on her at least to do something to her hair, and maybe help pick out more attractive glasses. It's so sad to see a young person let herself go like that. It's impossible even to guess how old she is. Do you know her name?"

"Karen Inman. I heard her ask for her mail general delivery. Why?"

"I don't know. Just wondering. Why she came here, I guess. She doesn't—fit. You know what I mean?"

"Uh-huh. No jeans, athletic shoes or hiking boots. Actually, Cecilia must have been thinking the same thing, because she asked her when she handed Karen her mail. Karen said she'd never been here before, just moved to Cedar

Harbor because she needed to get away from Seattle and heard it was a nice place."

"Does anyone know what she does for a living?"

"No, but she obviously doesn't keep working hours. Oh, by the way," Sue continued, "I was talking to that policeman while I was there, that new one?"

"Jake, you mean?" I noticed the faint blush that crossed her cheeks. Ahah! This was one time I would keep my mouth shut, though.

"Yes, Jake. Anyway, we spoke briefly about Lyle's murder, and I suggested he talk to you. There isn't anyone in town that knows more of the people and more of the history. I think," she smiled and her dimple showed, "that Jake's getting impatient with our esteemed Chief's prowess."

I grimaced. "Not surprising."

"Anyway, he said he would. I hope you don't mind?"

"Of course not. You know I like to talk."

"Well, I'd better be getting home," she said. "Come on, kids." She snared Jeff and Todd, which took a little doing, but between us we got them ensconced in the stroller and she left.

I glanced at my watch. Lunchtime. Well, just one more task before I went in to eat and take my short post-lunch nap. A perk of retirement.

First I went over to the knothole in the fence between my yard and Cyrus's. I peered through. All was clear. I picked up the milk carton with the slugs, then slowly pushed the loose board behind Cyrus's pole beans. I dumped and prodded until all the slugs I'd collected were out of the carton and on the ground.

"Good luck," I whispered to them. The first slug was already beginning to ooze toward his beans by the time I let the board sag back into place.

CHAPTER II

I glanced around the room appraisingly. Sue was right. I did know a surprising number of the people of our community. I'd met almost everyone in the Historical Society, of course, but probably half were also long-term friends or acquaintances. Most of those either had been pupils at Cedar Harbor Elementary or parents of one of those kids.

I flicked a look across the room at Karen Inman, where she sat alone. She was probably the only one there I hadn't been introduced to. I tried to envision the face and body stripped of the layers of fat. What color was her hair, really, before its unfortunate bleaching? And even her eyes were hard to see behind tinted glasses. She was perhaps forty, but it's so difficult to guess ages sometimes.

I suddenly realized that everybody in the room was looking at me expectantly. I searched my subconscious for what had last been said, and I groaned. Out loud, I'm afraid. That miserable Gloria Larson had just nominated me for president. "Oh, no," I said. "No, no, a thousand times no. Thank you, anyway." Even I knew the thanks were hollow sounding, but I didn't care. They'd tried to rope me into that unrewarding task just last year. Thank goodness I'd come today. I almost hadn't. I would much rather be planting those new roses I bought yesterday. But if I hadn't been on the spot, it would have been typical of Gloria to railroad the election through and I would have been president, just like that.

I could see the gaze of this year's president, Carrie Sanderson, search the room before it lit on Karen. Newcomers most often found themselves with the exalted title. I grinned. Karen wasn't stupid, I noticed. She refused to meet Carrie's gaze, just chewed on the knuckle of a forefinger. After a few seconds, Carrie reluctantly moved on to the next victim.

To heck with this. I gathered my things together, slid across the empty seats next to me and left. The organization was stagnant. Back when we thought we might actually pull together a museum project, it had been worthwhile, but now the programs were repetitive and boring. I'd come only out of a sense of loyalty. President, indeed. I'd done my stint, twice in fact. And turned it down at least twice since.

The meetings were held in the cramped back room of the library. I headed for the new book shelves and ran my fingers along them before I found a couple of mysteries that looked promising. I checked them out, then decided to stop in the bathroom before leaving. I set my books on the counter and headed into a stall.

Carrie must have found someone rather quickly to be president or given up, I realized as the outside door opened and several women came in. I stayed where I was. On the toilet, of course. I didn't relish facing recriminations.

I've been called names behind my back before, and it doesn't particularly disturb me. Nor did it surprise me that Gloria Larson was the culprit this time. "That Donna Galbreath," she sputtered. "She's nothing but a cantankerous, post-menopausal bitch!"

Post-menopausal I admit to, but I don't think I'm cantankerous—or a bitch—just because I'm not as patient with ignorant people as I once was and I absolutely cannot tolerate anyone of the *genus politico*. Gloria, unfortunately, is both. Ignorant as well as being one of those in any organization who are always pulling strings to put over their own private agendas. She'd love to be a full-fledged politician, but the only time she tried, when she ran for the school board, she was a dismal flop. Not surprising, considering her personality—missing. I always think personality implies something positive, don't you?

Besides, I don't know who she was trying to fool with that "post-menopausal" bit. As if she, herself, hasn't reached that plateau in life. She's my age, sixty, if she's a day, even if she dyes her hair that ridiculous dead black and, I suspect, periodically has her jowls lifted when she disappears for six weeks or so to visit her "niece." Besides, I've known her since she came to Cedar Harbor as a bride, and she certainly wasn't a schoolgirl then.

I sat there fuming until I heard the women leave. I really shouldn't let myself get that upset. Gloria was to be pitied, I reminded myself. She wasn't *quite* so difficult when I first knew her, back before her only child, a daughter, killed herself. That was a hard time for all of us. Little Mary was one of my students, and I have never forgotten the horror when it happened. It was difficult now, though, to picture Mary's face. She had been one of the quiet ones, self-effacing, with few friends. She hung around with someone for a while, though. I shook my head. Try as I might, I couldn't remember who it was. In the whole school year 'til her death, I never gained a clear picture of her personality. And I really tried. Those excessively withdrawn ones worry me, and of course I was tragically right that time.

I flushed the toilet, washed my hands and glanced at my watch. If I hurried, I'd still have time to plant those roses before I needed to fix the casserole I was going to make for the Women's Club potluck.

To my annoyance, as I walked up the street I could see a

police car parked in front of my house. It was Jake Santorini behind the wheel, at least, and not Billy Donniker. That was a relief. Hat in hand, Jake stepped out of the car when he saw me approach. "Good afternoon, Mrs. Galbreath," he said. "I wondered if you'd have a few minutes to talk to me? Sue Reilly recommended you."

"As a source of information?" I asked acerbically. Well, I guess I was, at that. I didn't need to be snappy. "Yes, I have time," I said, "but how would you feel about conducting this interview in my backyard while I garden?"

"Sounds good." A grin compressed his freckles.

I led him through my house and opened the door from the kitchen. "Make yourself comfortable," I said, "and I'll change clothes quickly and join you. How about some lemonade?"

"Sure," he said. "It's a thirsty day."

I opened the refrigerator, plunked some ice in two glasses and filled them from the pitcher. Handing one to him, I said, "Be with you in a minute."

When, dressed in grubbies, I stepped into my yard a few minutes later, I saw that he had made himself at home. He was sitting in a lawn chair next to the table, and had loosened his tie. Did that mean that this was an unofficial visit? I hoped so.

It was warm now that the morning overcast had cleared. I glanced around my yard, pleased at the general effect. The roses were in boisterous bloom, it being June, and the blend of perennials looked like a painting. I frowned. That delphinium could stand staking, and the daylilies that needed dead-heading hung like wet socks. I turned my back on them, sat in another lawn chair and reached for my own lemonade, which Jake had carried out. "What can I do for you?" I asked before I sipped.

20

He shrugged and spread his hands. "I'm not sure. I'm just groping. Groping for reasons why anyone would shoot Lyle Corrigan."

I snorted, to my embarrassment, almost spitting lemonade. I patted my lips with one of the napkins I'd snared on my way through the kitchen, then answered, "Your problem isn't going to be who might want to kill him, it's narrowing down the list."

He grinned ruefully. "I'd gathered that," he said. "By the way, I like that pink color of your house."

"Thank you." I brightened. "Not everyone feels that way." Cyrus, for one. He'd said it stuck out in the neighborhood like a whore at a church picnic. His house, predictably, is gray. Probably reminds him of some battleship he served on. "It's supposed to be rose-colored. I do think there are entirely too many gray houses these days, don't you?" Jake nodded, and I added modestly, "I painted it myself."

"You remind me of my mother," he said. "She does things like that."

What a pleasant young man. Well, he wasn't here to chat about the color of my house, so I said, "You want to know about Lyle. I knew him best when I ended up on the water board with him. He was chairman, you know."

He raised his eyebrows. "Why? If everyone disliked him."

I laughed. "You must be from the city. Nobody, but nobody, *wants* to be on a water board, and especially to be chairman—although, now that I think about it, there are exceptions. Lyle was probably one of them. If you're the sort who likes to throw your weight around, it's a perfect opportunity. Especially if you don't have a chance in your job.

"Cedar Harbor is unusual for a town its size in having a water board composed of volunteers," I explained to Jake. "When we incorporated, there were those who wanted to keep it that way. Foolish decision, in my opinion. Of course we do have that young man, Kirk Bentner, in charge of maintenance. But perhaps you know all this?"

Jake nodded, and shook the ice in his glass. I pushed my chair back. "Just a second, I should have brought the pitcher."

He bounced out of his chair. "Let me. If you don't mind my getting into your refrigerator."

I acquiesced. "How delightful to be waited on in one's own house." I sank back into the chair and, while he went inside, thought about the people who had tangled with Lyle.

"At the hardware store, Lyle was all politeness," I continued after Jake returned and we got lemonade taken care of. "He had to be, of course, and I'm sure it was a strain. There's so much competition with the mall out on the freeway. He knew how to run a business, I'll say that for him. But there were always stories . . . When he wanted to expand, rumor says he forced Carrie Sanderson out of business. She had a little place that sold local crafts. Nothing that drew customers from the city, you understand, but she was busy enough to make it and to stay occupied after she was widowed."

Jake frowned. "How did Lyle do that?"

"No one was ever exactly sure. Carrie lost her lease, though, and she'd been a good, steady tenant. Actually, as I recall, the landlord doubled her rent, and the rumor was that he let Lyle have it for the same price as she had paid. No way to prove that, of course. But rumors have a way of being true."

"Who was the landlord?"

"Al Parry, my neighbor down the street. He's the town pharmacist, you know. He's also on the water board."

"Why not blame Parry, then?"

"Oh, everyone did. But everyone was also convinced it

was Lyle's doing. What did Al get out of it? That's the question. Did Lyle pay him off with money, or something else . . . like silence?"

Jake thought that one over for a minute. I knew I didn't have to spell out what I meant. Lyle could have known all sorts of things about his old buddy, beginning with tax dodges.

I finished my lemonade and set the glass down. "Of course if I had been unfortunate enough to have married Lyle—which I'm glad to say I am much too intelligent to have ever considered—given the chance, of course, I'd have killed him long ago." I peered at Jake. "Where'd you get that red hair," I asked, "with a name like yours?"

He grinned. "Interestingly enough, redheads pop up in every nationality and race once in a while. I'm told my great-uncle had red hair before he lost it. The rest of my family are typical Italians—brown-eyed, brown hair."

Squinting, I said, "You got the eyes, though." Changing the subject back again, I asked, "You did take a look at Marie, I assume?"

He smiled, crinkles forming around those brown eyes. "You know I can't tell you what we're doing. I'm sorry that this has to be a one-way conversation. But—the police would have to be stupid not to look at family members."

"Yeah, but Chief Donniker's in charge."

The smile stayed on Jake's face but flattened slightly. He didn't respond to my remark. Tactful, too. "Tell me about Marie Corrigan," he did say.

"Mousy. Downtrodden. Had to ask Lyle for permission to sneeze."

"And the kids? You probably had them in school."

"I did." I leaned back, remembering. "Lyle, Junior had more gumption than his mother. He needed it. Nowadays, I think Lyle would have been hauled in for child abuse, but this was at least twenty-five years ago. I remember worrying, though, and when Junior took off, I was all for him. Although then I worried about his quitting school. Always hoped he finished high school at least, somewhere else. He had brains and he should have gone on to college. He was only seventeen when he left."

"And the daughter?"

"She took after Marie. I can't remember a lot about her. Always did her work, capably, too. But . . . she was mousy, no doubt about that. She was going to turn out just like Marie. Probably married a jerk, too. Funny, I don't recall ever hearing anything about what happened to either child in later years."

Something niggled at me about his daughter, but for the life of me, I couldn't think what it was. I glanced surreptitiously at my watch, but Jake saw me. He stood up. "Thanks, Mrs. Galbreath, that'll give me something to think about. I won't take any more of your time." He reached his hand across the table and I shook it.

"Call me Donna," I urged, "if you don't want to make me feel ancient."

After he left, I went into the garage for my shovel and gardening gloves. I knew exactly where I wanted the two roses to go. The first was to cover the new arbor I'd ordered from a catalog and managed to put together myself just yesterday, and the second was to climb the fence right near the loose board into Cyrus's yard.

Glancing at my watch again, I realized that there was no way I was going to get both planted and be ready for the Women's Club dinner. To heck with the dinner. They wouldn't miss my casserole—or me. I was meetinged out. Roses are much nicer than people, sometimes. Certainly nicer than Gloria Larson, who would undoubtedly be there with her famous home-made breadsticks. They're good, I'd give her that.

Usually I like other gardeners, but not Gloria. Of course she's a specialist, not a generalist like me who likes to try new plants, whose main goal is to produce harmonious beauty. Instead, Gloria grows rows of staked dahlias and propagates new ones. I think she's most interested in coming up with a perfect new specimen worthy of carrying her name and which she hopes will bring her fame and fortune.

As I dug, my thoughts kept jumping from the fiasco at the Historical Society this afternoon to my discussion with Jake. I wanted to think about the latter. Not that murder obsesses me, but it was a puzzle. Again, who, why, how? How had anyone who was an enemy of Lyle's lured him down to the dock in the middle of the night, for instance? The paper said the police had determined that was the most likely scenario, given the time of death. But, considering Chief Donniker's well-known thick-headed obtuseness, was even the time or place of death to be believed? Had he enough sense to bring in outside experts? I wish I knew more about police procedure, more than I've learned from reading mysteries.

And what did Jake mean when he said, "That will give me something to think about?" The word "that" somehow sounded singular. Was there a specific comment I'd made, something that gave him an idea to pursue?

But then, my mind jumped involuntarily to the meeting. Darn that Gloria. I don't know why I let her bother me. My thoughts drifted backwards, over everything that had been said and done. The speaker was mildly interesting, or would have been if I hadn't heard a dozen times before about how all traffic around Puget Sound was by boat back in the early days.

Then they discussed the usual. Should we put the same tired float in the Fourth of July parade, should we raise money in the same way with yet another pancake feed. I pictured all the people who had been there. The same faces, too, except for Karen Inman, with her folds of excess fat and straw-like, too-long hair.

She said she'd never been to Cedar Harbor before, but as I rocked back on my heels and concentrated, I wondered. I'd remember her distinctive appearance if I'd seen her at all recently, but what would she have looked like as a young person? Could she possibly be a former pupil of mine?

I shrugged. Even without the camouflage of hair, glasses and fat, it would be hard to recognize a student I'd had decades before and hadn't seen since. I always think anyone who looks that atrocious *is* truly hiding, even if only from herself.

And then it hit me. Literally. I teetered, and fell to my seat, squashing, unfortunately, my beautiful rose-colored Russell lupine. "Oh," I said. "I've got it! I remember!"

"What? What do you remember? About the murder?"

I looked up to see Cyrus, an avid expression on his face as he peered over the top of his fence. He had to be standing on the same bench as before.

"Do you always eavesdrop?" I asked, disgusted, as I picked myself up, brushed off the seat of my jeans and studied the unfortunate lupine.

"How can I help it, my dear neighbor?" he asked. "You do have such a penetrating, school-teacherish voice."

This time *I* growled.

CHAPTER III

The squeak of my gate opening alerted me. Cyrus was arriving in person. It seemed that lately all I'd seen of him was a disembodied head floating, as it were, above the fence line.

Cyrus probably was an impressive man in his officer's blues with all that gold braid. He's at least six feet, broad-shouldered and trim. He stays in shape. I've heard him grunting as he lifts weights in his yard when the weather's good. I assume he continues inside when it's bad. Discipline, that's his motto. He's always trying to give me the word. How was I lucky enough to have him buy the place next door when sweet old Mrs. Loman was dragged off to a nursing home by her uninterested daughter?

Cyrus even manages to discipline his hair. It's short, of course, probably fits the specifications of some Navy manual to a T, but it's still sandy colored, although a couple of shades lighter than his moustache. He hasn't lost any that I can tell. I can just hear him. "Hair," he orders, "don't go AWOL." Hell, he probably orders it not to grow, either. I've never noticed it being either particularly short or long.

"Your gate needs a shot of WD-40," he announced, swinging it slowly back and forth so that the noise that had never bothered me suddenly became excruciating.

"Cyrus," I said wearily, "must you do that?"

"What? Oh, that." He shut the gate slowly, with one last drawn-out squawk.

I'd hoped that he'd shut it with himself on the other side, but no such luck. However, I pride myself on not being rude. "Sit down," I suggested. He sat, although not until I did. I waited for him to speak first, even though I was quite sure I knew what he was here for. No reason to make being nosy easy for him.

"What did you remember? About Lyle's murder, I assume?" His blue eyes were sharp as he spoke, and I envisioned generations of underlings springing to please him.

"I'm not sure," I answered slowly, "exactly why what I remember concerns you."

"My dear Donna. Don't be difficult. You can't expect me not to be interested, after being a captive audience to your conversation with Officer Santorini."

"Oh, you know him?"

"Of course. A little matter. We disagreed on the speed limit on that stretch of road along the bluff."

I chortled, picturing the small red sports car Cyrus drives. Owning a car like that is asking for police attention. "Who won?"

"I'm not sure why that concerns you," he said, stuffy as ever.

We stared at each other for a second, but he broke first. Not surprising, since *my* information was of considerably more import than the question of how big a ticket he was likely to have earned.

His mouth twisted. "Does anyone ever win in an argument with a uniform and a badge? I got a ticket, of course, for speeding. Thirty-five is unreasonable on that stretch."

I almost tipped over the lawn chair laughing. "Too bad you weren't still in *your* uniform. How fast were you going?"

"Fifty-eight," he mumbled. "Now, your turn. The murder?"

"What I remember may not have anything to do with the murder, although . . ." My eyes narrowed as my memory kicked in again. Cyrus had the sense to remain silent. I was picturing a girl, one of my students of long ago. Sixth-grade girls run the gamut from childhood to maturity. This one had budding breasts and widening hips. She was taller at that stage than most of the boys, and they teased. She never responded, just blushed and hid her face behind dangling mud-colored hair. What I remembered now, though, was that when she was particularly stressed, she chewed her knuckles, to the point where they were often red and angry looking.

"Lyle's daughter," I said, "her name was Jolene. I suddenly remembered a habit she had. She chewed on the knuckles of her right hand."

"So?" Cyrus asked, staring intently.

"She's here. I haven't seen her in—let me see, something like sixteen or seventeen years—and she's come back. Have you seen that—well, to be kind, plump woman with the bleached blond hair who moved into the Satterburg cottage?"

"Yes-s," he hissed in understanding. "What are you going to do about it?"

I scratched my chin. "I haven't had time to think, you know that. But I suppose I must tell Jake."

"The young officer? I'm not on a first-name basis with him."

I chuckled. "I imagine you aren't. Nice young man, though, with brains, unlike . . ."

Cyrus nodded. Everyone knows about Billy. Funny, I hadn't thought of him as Billy for many years, until our little discussion the other day. But now I needed to concentrate on the matter at hand. "I'm sure the police will want to talk to her at the very least. But they're going to wonder, just as I do, why she's incognito."

"Suspicious," Cyrus agreed.

"Especially when her father—an obnoxious man—has been murdered. I hate to squeal, though. I feel sorry for her, even if it turns out . . ."

"Murder is never justified." Old stuffy surfacing again.

"You're a great one to talk. You made your living in a killing organization."

"Let's not get side-tracked into a discussion of ethics, shall we? Has no one else, to your knowledge, recognized this woman?"

I shook my head. "No one, at least as far as I've heard, and you know how gossip spreads around here."

"What about her family? She was here, as I recall, before Lyle was murdered. Did he know she'd come back?"

"OhmyGod," I said, "Marie."

"Marie?" He raised an eyebrow inquiringly.

"I forgot, you may not have met her. She does tend to— blend into the background. If she comes to gatherings at all. She's not a joiner. Lyle's wife. She *must* know Karen's Jolene, or Jolene's become Karen, or whatever. The girl couldn't possibly have expected to fool her parents. And she *was* here before Lyle was shot. I remember specifically seeing her—in fact," I said triumphantly, not because of what I remembered but because I had been able to do so, "I have a distinct picture in my mind of her *in* the hardware store. She was fussing over kitchen gadgets while I picked up some paint for my picnic table, and Lyle was behind the counter, and he didn't even glance in her direction."

Cyrus looked at me unblinkingly for a moment. "I think," he said slowly, "that you'd better take your memories to the police."

"I will. Right away." Standing, I said, "Goodbye for now, Cyrus, I'm sure our paths will cross again soon."

His moustache curled upward as he stood. "I'm sure they will. Always a pleasure."

I glanced at him sharply. Could it be that he *did* actually enjoy our encounters? Had I misjudged his sense of humor?

With a quick salute, he turned and left. The gate didn't squeak this time. He probably ordered it not to.

Sighing, I went inside to perform my distasteful duty. First I had to locate my glasses and find the number in the phone book. Such a nuisance, these days, since the telephone company tried to get helpful with all those colored sections. To my surprise, I found it the first place I looked. I dialed.

"May I please speak to Jake Santorini?" I asked. "It's—I think—important."

"He's not on duty today," the woman said. "Would you care to speak to Chief Donniker?"

I declined as politely as I could.

"Officer Santorini will be on duty tomorrow," the voice said, "although he'll only be in the office for a short period in the morning."

"Thanks," I said before hanging up.

I'd call him at home. Leafing through the book, I came to the S's. No Santorini. Darn, he probably hadn't been in town long enough or had an unlisted number. I wondered if Sue had it.

Was there any possible chance Marie didn't know about Jolene's return? Marie's sweet, the sort who's always fluttering in the kitchen and helping when she does come to neighborhood gatherings. What kind of a person would she have become, had she not married Lyle? Would she have developed her own personality? Most likely, from what I've read, she'd have married someone similar if it hadn't been Lyle. We do seem to determine our own fates.

Thumbing through the Women's Club Directory, I came

to her name. Marie Corrigan. And her number. Without stopping to think further, I dialed. "Marie?" I said, when the hesitant voice answered. "This is Donna Galbreath. Are you . . ." I'd started to ask if she was going to the Women's Club potluck, but then I realized that of course she wouldn't. I didn't know which would be worse in her circumstances, the commiseration or the gossip. "I need to talk to you," I blurted. "Will you be home, either now or this evening?"

"Well, now would be just fine," she said, "but I don't understand . . ."

"Neither do I," I told her firmly. "I'll be right over."

CHAPTER IV

The Corrigan house is one of the more ostentatious in Cedar Harbor. Not the most expensive, but there's a difference between homes designed to spill over the rocks of the coastline as unobtrusively as possible and one that has two-story pillars and a three-car garage festooned across the front. Those always look like car washes to me.

As I drove up the driveway and parked on all that asphalt, I reflected on the size of the place. It must have seemed empty with only two people rattling around after Jolene and Lyle, Junior left home, but now it must feel like an unoccupied Seahawks Stadium.

Marie opened the front door to my knock. "Come in, Donna," she invited. "This is—unexpected."

"Yes, well . . ." I shrugged. What she really meant was that I've never called on her before. I've been to the house, of course, when the Corrigans threw some large function. Not only have I never visited her, but just prior to the dinner hour isn't the usual time to drop in on someone. Well, as my mother used to say, "Needs must."

Marie eyed me in the silence, then, noticeably fluttering, suggested, "Shall we go in the living room?"

This was not to be a casual occasion, then, but she'd undoubtedly been entertaining a flow of callers with condolences in hand. Which reminded me of the formalities. "I did want to say I'm sorry about your loss." And her husband's death would be a loss to this woman, I was sure, regardless of what I thought of him. What I had to say now, I feared, wasn't going to make her feel any better.

"Thank you," she said. "Would you care for coffee or tea?"

Her brown peppered-with-gray hair was curled tightly and her gray eyes had deep circles under them. How I hated what I was going to do to her. I shook my head. "I hope this won't take long." She shot me a questioning look as I sat on a loveseat upholstered with striped mauve silk. It was slippery and hard. I felt as if my behind would slide off if I weren't careful.

"Marie," I began, "I haven't been introduced to her yet, but there's a new woman in town. Karen Inman." I watched her face as it hardened into lines that hadn't been there the last time I saw her.

"Yes?" was all she said. She wasn't going to make this simple.

"She's Jolene. Isn't she?"

"What makes . . . ?" She hesitated, then lowered her head, placing one hand over her eyes. I held my breath until she spoke again. I could barely hear the words. "How did you know?"

"A gesture she made. Somebody would have recognized her sooner or later, though. Why on earth is she hiding?" I blurted.

"She's not." Marie sat up straighter and looked me in the eye. "She's—well, I'm sorry to say my daughter is a very— disturbed young woman. She just doesn't want people to know she's come back to town."

Disturbed? I thought. How so? She certainly was able to function in a group. She'd appeared very pleasant, in fact, more outgoing than the Jolene I remembered. Nevertheless, her appearance did indicate a break with society's expectations, and certainly those her mother and father must have held for her. Jolene may have been shy as a young girl but she'd been given the usual advantages of braces on her teeth, piano lessons, nice though undistinguished clothes. I was remembering more about her all the time.

"Why doesn't she want people to know who she really is?" I asked. "She must have school friends still here as well as you and—her father." I gulped. Of course Jolene didn't have Lyle anymore and that was the nitty-gritty behind what I was here to say. "Why isn't she living with you?" I asked, gesturing toward the expansive upstairs.

"Donna," Marie said slowly, fingering the arm cover on the couch where she sat, "I'm surprised that you ask. My relationship with my daughter is—very private."

She had every right to think I was being rude. Normally her relations with Jolene wouldn't be my business. But this wasn't a normal occasion. "It would and could be private if not for one thing," I hastened to say. "Lyle's murder. Do the police know Jolene is here?"

"I assume not." She looked panicky. "Jolene is, as I said, disturbed, and it would be so difficult for her. Besides, one of Jolene's problems is, as you might guess, that she's become an habitual liar."

Liar? Why should I have guessed any such thing? The girl certainly hadn't been a story-teller in the sixth grade. Was Marie laying the groundwork for something that she didn't want Jolene to talk about now, like the fact that she had murdered her father?

"Marie," I leaned across the intervening space and put my hand over her nervously fidgeting one, "you must tell the police. They have to talk to family members."

"No, I can't." Her eyes widened in horror.

"Jolene, then," I said firmly. "Marie, if you—or Jolene—don't go to the police, I'll feel it's my duty to do so." I tried to say it as softly as I could.

She sank into herself, appearing to shrink to a person several inches shorter. "You would, wouldn't you?" she mumbled. "You always were—confident that you were right about everything."

"I'm not sure what you mean. But yes, I am confident about this, and yes, I will go to the police if you or Jolene don't do it first. I assume you will?"

Marie nodded, then appeared to shut me out totally.

I stood and patted her now-still hand. "I'm sorry, I truly am." With a last pat, I turned and departed, leaving a woman scrunched down in her chair who had suddenly become a withered old lady.

I inhaled again. The driveway was lined with roses, carefully spaced and pruned. I should have been smelling them, but there was no fragrance in the air. The roses were all those over-bred, odorless creations of modern science. Sterile. Just like the house.

I shivered, and noticed that it had become noticeably cooler while I was inside. The sky was no longer totally blue, as it had been consistently this drought-prone year. Streaky clouds hinted at a change in weather. What a relief that would be. I was glad when I let myself into my own, cozy home. It suited me, even if it was simple. At least one could smell the flowers here.

I tossed and turned after I went to bed that evening, worrying. Worrying about, and for, Marie and Jolene. They didn't deserve what was happening to them. Lyle's problem, whatever it had been, was of his own making, I was convinced. Even if that problem involved a family member. What a euphemism I was using, I realized. Problem. What I meant was, even if Marie or Jolene had shot Lyle, he had probably brought it on himself. But then, much as I hated to agree with something Cyrus had said, there is no excuse for murder.

A long unheard noise made me lift my head. The hints of the clouds had been correct. It was actually raining. With the sound of steady drops hitting my patio roof, I rolled over once more and went to sleep.

The rain had stopped by morning, but leaves glistened and sparkled. Some of the flowers drooped, but they'd recover with a burst of new energy. Somehow, human watering never accomplishes what God's does. The slugs would be loving it, too. My first chore of the day would be gathering a new batch for Cyrus. I chuckled in anticipation.

I was no longer chuckling after I started collecting. How on earth could there be so many? Gray, spotted gray, brown slugs, yellow and black banana slugs. Someday I would have to take a book out of the library and learn more about them other than the fact I knew so well that they are voracious feeders. Where had the banana slugs come from? They usually frequent woodlands, not flower gardens and, I know, perform the very useful function of helping dead vegetation decompose.

I gathered all I could find and it took me some time. I wasn't particularly careful as I pushed the board of the fence. Cyrus wasn't home. I'd heard the red sports car leave. I had so many slugs, I decided, that he might notice something awry if I dumped them all in the usual spot. I divided my harvest, and dropped some over the top of Cyrus's fence as well, one group near his herb garden and the other to head toward the Brussels sprouts.

I went to the P.O. late in the afternoon, missing the usual rush of Cedar Harborites that occurs shortly after ten-thirty when the mail comes in and is distributed to our boxes. A postcard with a picture of a stave church in Norway was on top. I knew it was from my dear friend, Alice Pierce, who retired from teaching this year. She'd wanted me to accompany her on a tour of Europe, but that had been impossible. "You'd love Norway," I deciphered, "although the mountains don't match ours."

I leafed through the rest of the stack. Good. There was a letter from my daughter, Roberta, who lives with her husband in New York City and works in publishing. About as far away geographically as she could be, but still, she wasn't so different from me. She'd majored in English, my favorite subject. Roberta could be a good teacher, and maybe she would some day when she got tired of the big city.

As I skimmed her letter, I shamelessly eavesdropped on the other post office patrons, but no one was talking about the murder. Apparently there were no new developments. Maybe it was too soon for word to get out about Jolene, regardless.

The next morning I made a point of being at the P.O. at ten-thirty, and I lingered instead of making my usual dash back to my box and then out. One can waste so much time in conversation with uninteresting people if one is not careful, I'd decided shortly after my retirement. Of course it's a good place to see people one does want to talk to. I was pleased to see Carrie Sanderson walk in the front, her sunglasses pushed on top of her white curls, her athletic suit sleek and unmussed.

"Hi, Donna," she called, detouring in my direction. "Missed you at the Women's Club the other night, and I've been meaning to call you."

"I know," I said. "I mean, I know I should have come, but . . ."

"But you didn't want to after Gloria Larson's unfortunate gaffe in the bathroom."

"Well, that wasn't it, but—how did you know I was in there?"

"I saw your feet when I leaned over to see which stalls were empty. You had on your handsome Birkenstock sandals. It was too late to shut her up. Gloria can be such a bitch herself, but she's a good worker. I don't think she means to be so . . ."

"Rude?"

"I was going to say caustic."

"Hmmm. Well, you did your usual good job as president. Did you find anyone for the task next year?"

She shrugged, the dappled pink material on her shoulders rippling. "I think we'll wait a bit and hit Marie. She'll need something to do. I remember how it was after I was widowed. You must remember what that was like."

"Not exactly. I had to figure out, fast, how I was going to make a living. That kept me occupied. I had Roberta to raise, too."

Her eyes widened. "I didn't realize. Or think. I'm sorry, Donna."

"No problem. It was a long time ago."

"Yes, well, to get back to the subject of the presidency, let's face it, if we don't get one before fall, it's no killing matter." He mouth twisted wryly. "I didn't mean a pun. I'm sorry. I'm really putting my foot into it today. So tasteless."

"But apropos. Carrie, I noticed you skipped over that new young woman, Karen Inman?" I was pleased with myself for finding an excuse to interject Marie's daughter into the conversation.

"Ye-es. She definitely was avoiding my eyes, but then so was everyone else. It just seemed too soon to ask her. I mean, if she were the sort to jump into our activities right away, I might have done, but she does keep to herself. She shows up at meetings, but no one has gotten to know her. And the president needs to interact with members. I thought in another year . . ."

I nodded, even though I suspected the chances of the woman's being president next year were nil. At the very least, if she were around to be president and not in jail, it would not be as Karen Inman.

"I have to dash," Carrie said, "but let's get together for lunch. How about, um, Tuesday, at the Harbor Inn? It's been a long time since we've just visited."

"Tuesday sounds good." We both have acquired enough wisdom with our advancing years to avoid time-consuming cooking for luncheon guests. Much simpler just to meet in a restaurant.

Hmmm. If Carrie didn't know about Jolene yet, then probably the word wasn't out. I watched her leave and I eavesdropped on a few more conversations, none of which was about the Corrigan family. Was I going to have to take action?

The decision was made for me when I noted a black and white cruiser pulled up in front and I spotted Jake's red hair. He was speaking to Sue. The expression on his face made it evident that they were not discussing police business. Good. Sue's evident attraction was not one-sided. When she continued on up the street, I went outside. I'd allowed plenty of time for Marie or Jolene to go to the police.

"Jake," I said, meeting him on the sidewalk in front, "I need to talk to you. Privately." I glanced around, feeling like a criminal myself, trying to figure out how to avoid being overheard. "I know. I'll head on home, and if you could just happen to drive by, we can chat for a minute as if it were an accident."

"Sure thing, Donna," he said, then disappeared inside.

I strode away before I could become entangled with anyone else. Jake was fast. I'd barely turned the corner off of Main and onto Beach Drive before he pulled up alongside me and rolled down the window on the passenger's side. "Do you want to get in?" he asked. "I could give you a lift."

I shook my head. "It'll just take me a second. Have you— the police department, I mean—had a call from either Marie Corrigan or that new young woman in town, Karen Inman?"

"No. Should we have?"

"Yes. I remembered something that could be important. I told Marie that if she didn't call you I would, but . . ."

He interrupted. His brown eyes had suddenly become cold, which is hard to do with brown eyes. "You went to someone else with something important that you remembered before you told us?"

"Well, put that way—yes. I thought it was their information to pass on."

"Donna, this is an investigation of a murder. May I ask exactly what it was that you remembered and when this discussion took place with Marie Corrigan?" His voice now was cold, too.

I felt like one of my sixth-graders must have when I was chewing him out. "It was night before last, about five o'clock," I said, "that I confronted Marie with the fact that I was sure Karen Inman was, in fact, her daughter, Jolene."

"You're positive?"

"I wouldn't say so if I weren't," I answered, miffed.

"And Marie Corrigan admitted to you that this young woman was her daughter?"

I nodded.

"Was there anything else you remembered that you're neglecting to tell us?"

41

I didn't think he needed to speak in such a sarcastic tone, but perhaps this wasn't the time to bring that up. I shook my head. "No, that's it."

With a glare quite unlike the Jake I have known, he rolled the window back up, did a fast U-turn and disappeared down the street.

If I thought Jake was angry, it was nothing compared to the boiling ill-humor displayed by Chief Donniker when he called on me the next morning.

He didn't even come in. He stood on my porch where anyone could hear and he yelled.

"I thought someone who'd been a teacher would have more sense," he said.

"But I . . ."

"Do you realize what you've done?"

"Well, no, but I . . ."

"What you've done," he said, narrowing his eyes in approved cop fashion and waving a pointed forefinger under my nose, "is alerted that woman. Lyle's daughter is missing. She's taken off."

"Oh, boy," was all I could say.

"You are an interfering female," he said, "and you . . ."

At that point I tuned him out other than to note that he'd increased his vocabulary considerably since the sixth grade, although not all the words he used would have been in a school text.

Suddenly, I had a flash of insight. I interrupted his commentary referring to something about the number of brain cells I had. I do believe, underneath it all, that he was enjoying telling off a teacher who had not made his sixth-grade year particularly pleasant.

"Has the thought crossed your mind," I asked, "that

maybe she didn't make the decision to take off? That instead, someone wants her missing?"

That shut him up.

CHAPTER V

Wouldn't you know that Cyrus heard the whole thing? Undoubtedly, the Grissoms to my north and the Moores across the street listened in also, not to mention Chuck, the UPS man, who was standing, mouth agape, waiting to deliver a package of gardening goodies I'd ordered from Smith and Hawken.

By the time Chief Donniker whirled around, leaped into his patrol car and took off with spinning wheels and I'd signed for the package, Cyrus came strolling up my front walk. Grinning.

"Well, well. Guess both of us are unpopular now with the local police establishment," he said.

"If you heard it all, you must realize that I'm in hot water only because I followed *your* advice to go to the police about Jolene."

"As *I* recall, it was a consensus decision. Anyway, do I gather that you delayed this little visit to the police department?"

He *was* enjoying himself.

"Goodbye, Cyrus," I said firmly, stepping inside my house. "Always a joy to speak with you." I didn't give him the pleasure of hearing me slam the door.

Life had been so peaceful before Cyrus showed up that dreadful August day last year. I'd been anticipating meeting my new neighbor, since I've always been on good terms with those on both sides of my place.

The first sign of trouble was the surveyors sighting down the line between our houses. It was obvious right away that they were envisioning a line considerably inside my picket fence. I ignored the thought, though, complacent fool that I was.

The next thing I knew, Cyrus knocked on my front door and introduced himself. He was all business. No fooling around with amenities. He declined my offer to come in. "You do realize," he said, "that your fence is on my property?"

"Why, no, I didn't," I said, still innocently assuming that we would have the neighborly relations that I was accustomed to.

"It is. The front corner is okay, but then the fence diverges until it's almost three feet out of line at the back corner." He began unfolding a large map.

"Hmm," I said, only glancing at the map as I wondered what he thought I was supposed to do about it.

"What I suggest, if you have no objection, is that I replace the fence, at my expense of course, and correct the line so there is no problem in the future."

Sounds reasonable, I thought. Hah. My first mistake was acquiescing and signing the agreement he handed me without going and getting my glasses first. The second was telling myself what a pleasant, generous new neighbor I had acquired.

My third mistake was leaving town. The Retired Teachers were having a conference, and I cheerfully went to join my compatriots, not expecting any changes in the few days I was to be gone. Well! When I returned, it was to find that Cyrus had ripped out my picket fence and replaced it with the Berlin Wall. Worse yet, to do so, he slashed and crushed, wrecking mature flowering shrubs that had lined my picket fence. He took out the native trees on his side that provided the right

45

conditions for my shade garden in the back corner of my lot. And, the new fence was so high that I now had shade conditions elsewhere for plants that needed and expected sun.

I'd stormed over to his house. "Won't you come in?" he inquired. Always superficially polite, that's Cyrus.

I myself didn't bother with politeness this time. "What is that—that monstrosity you have erected between our houses?"

"Why, my dear lady," he said, "that is the fence that I asked you about and which you agreed to—in writing, I might add. I think it's quite handsome."

"What does your wife think about it?" I asked, sputtering.

His back stiffened and his eyes grew remote. "I don't have a wife."

"That figures," I said.

The feud between us had begun.

I really must watch what Cyrus does to my blood pressure, I thought to myself now as I stormed through the house. Although actually, my pounding heart and flushed face could be blamed equally on Chief Donniker and Cyrus. I put the kettle on to make some tea. Something so soothing about cradling the warm cup and sipping the brew, even if it does contain caffeine.

So much for trying to assist the police. Even Jake Santorini was angry at me. I'd thought I could go to him if I needed to discuss anything with a policeman, but now that was out. At least I'd given Billy something to think about. One would suppose a policeman would be thoughtful enough to ponder and worry when a witness disappeared, rather than assuming that said witness was the villain. Not our Chief, apparently. I wondered if it had occurred to Jake that Jolene might conceivably be a victim rather than a culprit?

Of course, I didn't know that this was a fact. I poured the

tea to steep, and sat down at the kitchen table to assess the information I had.

Usually just glancing around my domain brings me peace. My kitchen table is square, an old cherry piece that my parents bought from a dressmaker during the Great Depression. You can still see the fine dotted lines her seam marker incised. I had new cabinets put in as a gift to myself when I retired, and they're cherry, too. So warm and welcoming. Through the years, as I double-paned the windows to help with the ever-increasing heat bills, I've enlarged them. I love the view into my lovingly tended flowerbeds.

But today nothing helped my mood. I felt surly, that was the only word for it. Cyrus had better not cross my path again soon.

The tea should be ready. I brought the cup back to the table. Maybe the fact that the day was gray wasn't helping. The papers are full of stories of people who succumb to depression induced by the cloud cover so often typical of the Seattle area. But, no. I've never been bothered by clouds or rain before, in fact, I rather like them.

I wished the Chief had taken the time to be more explicit. How did they know Jolene was missing, rather than just off on a trip? Or had he jumped to conclusions? I sat and sipped and thought. It was obvious I wasn't going to find out anything from the police department. The one other person who should know was Marie. Did I dare call her?

My hand reached for the phone. It couldn't do any harm. Marie was already unhappy with me. But wait. Would she, like Chief Donniker, blame me because Jolene was gone? I fumed, drinking my tea, which wasn't having its desired effect.

I glanced up at the framed photo of my husband, Bob. He'd always been the one who made most of the decisions before he died. Good decisions, too, except for the one we made jointly that I quit studying at the University and have a baby. Life had been so much more difficult when Bob died a few short years later than it would have been if I'd completed my education first. He was so young. The face looking at me now that of just a boy. I'd learned to make decisions. I'd had to. Defiantly, I again reached for the phone. If Marie was blaming me, my calling wouldn't make anything worse.

The voice that answered was so low and weak in volume that I wasn't sure who it was. "Marie, is that you?" I asked.

"Yes . . . It's me. Donna?"

At least she hadn't hung up on me. Yet. "Yes," I admitted. "Marie, I'm sorry. I heard . . ." I couldn't go on.

"That Jolene is missing? It's true."

I realized, suddenly, that a lot of my distress was because deep down, I *did* feel responsible. If I had gone directly to the police instead of to Marie, Jolene of the bleached hair and overweight body would still be in the Satterburg cottage, having told her story, or would be in jail. Alive, anyway. That she wasn't, was what I feared.

"I—I shouldn't have interfered."

"No," Marie said, "you shouldn't have."

"I wish greatly that I hadn't." That wasn't strictly true. My perhaps overblown conscience wouldn't have let me ignore the situation once I realized who Karen really was, but I should have gone directly to the police.

"I wish she'd never come back," Marie said, bitter-sounding.

"How do you know—I mean, did she tell you she was leaving or—or pack, or anything?"

"No. Nothing. She's just not there. She was supposed to come over for lunch and she didn't show up. No phone call or anything. Her purse is missing, the police say, and she with-drew her money that she'd put in the bank under her other name."

"How much?" Again I wondered where Jolene got her money. An allowance from her parents?

"Donna . . ." Her voice held a warning note. I'd stepped over the line that she had drawn, protecting what she didn't want known.

"Had you told her I knew?"

"Of course. You left me no alternative." And then she began to cry.

Oh, boy. Now I felt really guilty. Anger I had been pre-pared for. But tears . . . "Forgive me. If there is anything I can do . . ."

"It's not your fault," she said through her weeping. "I didn't mean what I said. You were right. Jolene shouldn't have hidden who she was after her father died. She should have known the police would want to talk to her. The whole thing's her fault, for—for coming back and lying."

"Marie, have you told the police she'd been lying? I mean, about other things than who she was?"

Snuffle, snuffle. "Yes. That's why they think—they think she killed Lyle."

I opened my mouth to ask what, exactly, she'd been lying about, but then I realized asking wouldn't do any good. If Marie had been reluctant to tell me why Jolene hadn't moved into the large house and whether she'd had a lot of money in the bank, then Marie certainly wasn't going to explain Jolene's lies.

I made a few more apologies, and genuinely repeated my offer of assistance if there was anything I could do, then hung up. I'd have liked to ask her, too, who else knew I'd been going to go to the police. For that matter, had anyone else known that Karen was really Jolene before I cottoned onto her? It was certainly a possibility.

I'd learned a little, but I wasn't likely to find out anything more until it was public knowledge. Certainly, neither Jake nor the Chief was going to confide in me. In a sense, Marie was right when she implied that what happened to the Corrigan family was none of my business. It wasn't, other than the fact that I'd found Lyle's body, and then inadvertently been drawn into the mess by my rather acute memory. Now I was just going to have to try to put it out of my mind and get on with my own affairs.

I managed to follow that advice until Tuesday when I met Carrie Sanderson for lunch. The Harbor Inn was full of tourists, the day being a scrumptious one in June. Fortunately, Carrie had made reservations, and we had a table at a window overlooking the marina and bay. Such a joyous sight to watch colorfully dressed boat people maneuver their playthings for a day of fun. When the boats are going out, the seagulls always seem extra cheerful, too, knowing they'll find snacks from lunches and fish drawn by exotic baits. I enjoy birdwatching but I've never learned to differentiate the various gulls. A particularly beautiful pure white one, though, floated down and settled on a piling to watch the proceedings as we studied our menus.

"I never have to look at the menu long here at the Inn," Carrie said. "I always have their chowder and alder-smoked salmon."

"But then you miss the fried clams," I pointed out.

She nodded. "You can't have everything, but," she flashed that appealing smile of hers, "we could share, if clams are what you're going to choose."

"Good idea," I agreed, and we placed our orders with the

waitress who, naturally, had been one of my students a few years back.

Talk swung to the Corrigan family almost immediately. On impulse, I asked Carrie, "What was the story when Lyle expanded the hardware store and you lost your lease? I really didn't hear details at the time."

"What's to hear?" she answered, a bitter expression erasing her normally cheerful one. "Al Parry proposed doubling my rent, and I was barely clearing enough to make staying in business worthwhile. There wasn't any point in struggling on."

"Couldn't you have moved the shop?"

"Where? My location was perfect, right on Main and so close to the Inn. Tourist traffic kept me going. Locals don't buy that many crafts and souvenirs and gifts, you know."

"No, I don't suppose they do. But what about the report that Lyle was behind getting you dumped?"

Carrie shrugged. "He's the one who profited by my leaving. He expanded his store, his business probably increased by a third and I was out in the cold."

I noticed that she hadn't exactly answered my question. "Was it true that Al gave the space to him for what he'd been charging you?" I probed.

"I don't know. At least—I can't prove it."

The police could, it occurred to me.

"I have no doubt that Lyle was behind the whole thing," she said, her mouth twisted with dislike. "Needless to say, I haven't set foot in his store since. A small triumph, but one that makes me feel better."

"What about Al? Sounds as if it was as much his fault. Do you patronize The Drugstore?" I asked.

She laughed grimly. "You couldn't pay me enough. And most of my friends refuse to shop in their stores, either."

I felt a stab of guilt. Boycotting the two hadn't occurred to me, and I'd been a friend, although not a close one, of Carrie's for many years. My thoughts must have showed on my face, because she said, "Don't worry about it, Donna. I know you had to get along with both Lyle and Al since you were on the water board with them."

"If you can call what I do, 'getting along.' Our relationship is—was—more like a face-off between a coon and a cat. A large cat. Me."

Her mood lightened, which was my intent. I went on, "Lyle and Al were such buddies, two of a kind. I suppose, difficult as it may be to imagine, that Al misses Lyle."

Carrie shook her head. "They used to be buddies," she said, "but I'm quite sure they hadn't been lately. I'd heard stories . . ."

I had my mouth open to ask her what she'd heard when the town siren went off. Like everyone else, we stopped talking and waited to see what it was all about. In a few seconds, whatever it was—the aide car or fire truck—left the station up the street and headed down Main toward us. Then, I could tell from the sound, it turned along Beach Drive in the other direction from the route to my house. I relaxed, as did most of the other diners. Conversation began to buzz again.

Just then, Alissa, our waitress, brought our chowder. I changed the subject then on purpose. No point in ruining our lunch. The meal was superb, as usual, and I certainly wasn't going to need dinner.

Alissa's face was flushed as she hurried toward us with our check. "Did you hear?" she asked. "My boyfriend was on his bike, and he lives up on Whale Way at the other end of Beach. It's the only way for him to get to town, and he saw the ambulance. His brother's a paramedic and . . ."

"Alissa," I interrupted just as I had many times in the sixth grade, "please get to the point."

She wasn't insulted, being used to me even if she had never learned to be concise. "Well, I was going to say that he had to come by the Corrigan house and he saw them coming out."

I shook my head in exasperation. "Who?"

She blinked a couple of times before she answered. "Mrs. Corrigan," she said, her mouth round with excitement. "Something's happened to Mrs. Corrigan!"

CHAPTER VI

The red light was blinking on my answering machine when I got home. I pushed the play button, then groaned when I heard the deep bass tones of Al Parry. "I'm calling a board meeting," he said. "It's important. Be there." That was Al Parry, all right. He hadn't identified himself and he didn't need to. "Seven-thirty tomorrow night. My place." And then, to my surprise, he added, "Bring your suit." Well, well. I was finally being invited to try the famous hot tub.

What could be so important that he'd call a special meeting on such short notice? For that matter, why was Al the one calling the gathering in the first place? I didn't recall anyone naming him chairman after Lyle's death. Although much as I hated to admit it, the choice might be logical. There were only four of us left. Cyrus, who's too much of a newcomer, Michael Jarvis, who's too much of a wimp, Al, who's too much of a jerk, and me. I, of course, am too much of an independent, one who no longer cares if she steps on toes. I decided, rationally, that the jerk would get my vote. Still, one does hate to see assumptions made.

I'd never seen the notorious hot tub, even though Al lives in the next block, but on the water side. It would be interesting, although, on reflection, seeing Al *in* the hot tub might be more so. Al likes the good life. Someday I expect to hear that he has gout, if it's true that overindulging in food and alcohol causes the strange disease. All that consumption is reflected, in Al's case, by a portly build that couldn't possibly look good in swimming trunks.

Which made me think of my own appearance on this momentous occasion. Hmmm. Luckily I'm gardening tough, but beginning to be spotted with old lady blotches, much as I hate to admit it. They do seem to appear most on people who have had dark hair, it seems to me. My own is now mostly gray, but it used to be brown and I spent hours in the sun as a teenager seeking the elusive perfect tan.

My mind suddenly jumped, as quick minds tend to do. Marie Corrigan wasn't worrying about age spots or how her body would appear in a swim suit. Likely her body was being examined intimately about now, if hospitals are still like the last one I was in, when a much-too-young man stripped me of my gall bladder. What was wrong with Marie? Had she had a heart attack, precipitated by the stress of Lyle's death and Jolene's disappearance? Had she had an accident? Had she, I worried with a sudden sinking feeling, been attacked? Was there a vendetta against the Corrigan family? Or, perhaps worse yet, was I wrong about Jolene and she had indeed indulged in patricide and attempted matricide?

What a rash of irrational thoughts, I decided. How could I find out why the ambulance was called to whisk Marie off to the hospital?

I sat in front of the phone, baffled. Who could I call that would have inside information? No one, that's who. At least no one who would be likely to tell me anything before those in authority were good and ready. If I knew Cedar Harbor, though, by tomorrow when I made my daily trip to the post office, the tidings would be on everyone's lips.

Shrugging, I went to change my clothes and go do something worthwhile in the garden. I felt like vigorous shoveling but June isn't the time of year for that, at least this year, with its stifling temperatures. The rain last week cooled things down for a while, but the thermometer had again ascended into the uncomfortable zone of the mid-eighties, with worse forecast for later in the week. I'd begin by sprinkling my poor former shade garden to give the plants relief. I'd been moving them to more salubrious locations as fast as I could, but it would be a death sentence to transplant in this weather.

I'd barely started the hose when Cyrus showed up. This time I groaned out loud without any guilt. The man has a talent for being irritating. Not that he'd done anything irritating yet, but that he would was a foregone conclusion.

I was right. "Donna," he began in a long-suffering tone, "don't you ever learn? It's precisely," he studied his watch as he held up his arm, "two-thirty in the afternoon, *not* your day . . ."

"Cyrus," I said wearily, "if you have something important to say, say it. And leave. I don't feel like submitting to your guff today." I turned my back.

"Oh," he said, "something special wrong to make us touchy?"

"Just a little. Marie Corrigan was hauled off to the hospital, and I don't know why. *And* my primroses and my bugbane are suffering from the heat because their necessary shade was abruptly removed on, as I recall, August sixteenth of last year. Is that enough?"

"I *am* sorry to hear about Mrs. Corrigan. That family has had entirely too much grief. My sympathies are with them."

I swung my head around. His expression *was* distressed. "I'm surprised to hear you say that, Cyrus."

"Why? I know about grief."

Chagrined, I blushed. I *had* been rude. And I really knew so little about Cyrus. I released the pistol grip on the nozzle so that it shut off, and turned around. "Would you care to sit down?" I asked.

Without answering, he drew out a chair, and then another. We both sat.

He came right to the point, as usual. "I was wondering," he said, "if you know what this water board meeting is about. Since you always know what's going on."

I wasn't sure whether the latter remark was intended to be an insult or a compliment. I decided to ignore it. "This time I don't. I only know what was on my answering machine, which was the usual blustering Al Parry."

Cyrus shook his head. "A difficult man."

Well. We agreed about something. Although, I didn't see how any sane person could think otherwise. The surprise is that Al is able to remain in business in a town such as Cedar Harbor. That's probably because he mostly stays behind the counter filling prescriptions, ably as far as I know, while his wife, Noreen, a pleasant, even charming woman, deals with the public.

"I heard something today," I began. "I didn't follow up on it and I should have. Do you know anything about a falling out that Al and Lyle may or may not have had?"

"Didn't you notice the coolness between them at that last meeting before Lyle died?"

I shook my head. I hadn't. How could I have missed something that an insensitive man like Cyrus picked up on? I thought back to that last meeting. We'd gone over the usual picky stuff and then the discussion had turned to the large housing development that had been proposed earlier by Mark Gasper. With my photographic memory, I envisioned the scene. Al had brought the subject up, as I recalled, and, yes, Lyle had been irritated. He'd controlled himself, but I had a clear picture of his face, pinched with annoyance.

"That project's dead," he'd said.

Al had shrugged. "I think you're making a mistake."

Mistake? In retrospect, I wondered what he was referring to, exactly. Lyle wasn't God. He hadn't had a divine decision-making role in the county's establishment of a moratorium. There were rumors, of course, as I had told Jake back before I was blackballed or exiled or whatever, that Lyle did have more to do with stopping the development than he should have had as president of a small-town water district committee.

The subject had changed, then, to more mundane matters.

"I see you've again remembered something." Cyrus looked at me quizzically.

I shook my head to clear it and said, "Not really. Just recalling that meeting, and I think you're right. I wonder whether I should . . ."

"Tell the police?"

"Well, that was what I was thinking, of course, but . . ." This time I shook my head firmly. "No. Not anymore. I hate to say I mustn't become involved, but I'm afraid that decision has been forced on me. I did inform Jake about the matter of the development, and it's up to him."

Cyrus stood. "Not much to tell, really," he muttered. "But I don't have any doubt that the two were no longer friends. Well, if you don't have any insider's knowledge about tomorrow night's meeting, I'll leave you to your gardening."

"Insider's knowledge, hah!" I said.

At seven twenty-five, I gathered together my bag with towel, etc., my purse, and a light jacket in case there were evening breezes off the Sound. I wore my bathing suit. The new one I'd purchased at Lander's in town that morning. How fortuitous that they'd been having a sale. I rather thought that I didn't look too bad in the cherry-colored one-piece. For an old lady, that is. I'd covered it, of course, with dark slacks and a knit shirt. I assumed that a meeting that included hot-tubbing would be casual.

Other than finding the suit, which had reached out from the window of Lander's as if it had determined that it should belong to me, my trip to town this morning was a wash-out. No mail and no information. Not strictly so. Of course there was junk mail and, in hindsight, junk information. The only thing that I gathered from conversing with several people was that the hospital had been remarkably reticent about Marie's condition, other than that she was holding her own.

So, I locked my front door, admiring the deep rose color I'd painted it to complement the rest of the house, and headed up the street to Parry's. Noreen was the one to greet me.

"Donna," she said, hugging me, "it's been too long."

I hugged back, although I thought the gesture was a little extravagant for two women who seldom socialize. I had nothing against Noreen except her choice in a mate.

"Go right on back," she said, leading me to a sliding door that opened onto an expansive deck. "Unless you need to change." She glanced at my bag. "You did bring a suit?"

"I have it on. Thanks."

The doorbell rang just then and she excused herself. I hovered to see who had arrived, but when I heard Michael Jarvis's bland tones, I went ahead. Al and Cyrus were already in the tub, I could see.

It was going to be a magnificent evening. Enough low clouds hung on the horizon to effect a beautiful sunset, when the time came. Already there was a pink cast to the sky. Al's property was high bank, so only the distant water could be seen across an expanse of lawn. A green lawn. How was he keeping it like that on our watering regimen? Even without Cedar Harbor's rigid schedule, there's an unofficial pact these days in the Puget Sound area to let lawns go. When I was a child, no one dreamed the day would come that this part of the country would be anything but green. Unlike Cyrus, though, I would keep my thoughts to myself. Besides, my complaining would make me the pot that was calling the kettle black.

As I stood, musing and admiring the view, Al eased himself from the tub. Oh, boy. I had to shift my eyes toward Cyrus to keep amusement from showing on my face. Cyrus's eyes twinkled as they met mine, so obviously that odious man knew what I was thinking.

Al's body should never see the light of day. Especially in the skimpy suit he chose to wear. He'd clearly worked on acquiring a deep bronze color, because a thin strip of white showed where his bathing suit had shifted from the exertion of extricating himself from the tub. The color of his skin did nothing to help the overall effect. Or maybe it did. The thought of the same body in pale tones was enough to make me choke. Poor Noreen.

Bob had had a beautiful body, one that I'd enjoyed in every way. If he had lived, he'd have never allowed himself to deteriorate as Al had done.

"Aren't you going to join us?" Al asked.

"Oh. Oh, yes," I said, flustered at the direction my thoughts had been flowing.

As Al turned to greet Michael, I set my things down next to a chair and stripped off my pants and shirt. When my gaze swung toward the pool, it was to note Cyrus, leaning back and resting one arm along the side as he studied me appraisingly. With a slight smile.

"Like what you're seeing?" I asked in an all too common acerbic tone as I wished I weren't blushing to go along with it.

"Indeed," Cyrus said.

Grrr.

Fortunately I was saved from saying something I might regret by Michael's cheery voice. "That water looks *delightful*," he said, already ripping off his shirt.

As long as I, and everyone else it appeared, was analyzing bodies, I studied him as I slid into the tub as far from Cyrus as possible. Nothing wrong with Michael's shape. He even flexed a bicep before he stepped down to join us. He's one of those who make up the crowds no one is noticed in. Pleasant features and manners, nothing memorable. If I'd seen him unclothed, though, I would have remembered him. Somehow, I'd never noticed his build when he was in his usual business suit. I wasn't even sure what he did for a living. Accounting, or something like that.

Michael sat across from me, next to Cyrus. I realized my error when Al sidled into the pool, raising the level considerably, and settled next to me. As unobtrusively as possible, I began to inch my behind toward Cyrus. The old phrase about being between the devil and the deep blue sea came to my mind. Appropriate, except that I was also *in* the deep blue sea.

"Thought we could settle business amicably," he said, gesturing expansively, "if we're all relaxed. We're neighbors, of course, and . . ." He stopped speaking and raised his gaze to the sliding door, where Noreen was shepherding a man out onto the deck.

Oh-oh, I thought. I flicked a glance at Cyrus, who raised one of those old-man bushy eyebrows sardonically.

Al removed himself again, precipitating a tidal wave.

"Mark," he said in a gratingly pleasant tone, "come join these folks. I was just beginning to explain tonight's agenda."

Mark Gasper, the infamous developer, a nice man who wanted to provide affordable housing and helped widows of former employees, if you believed Sue Reilly. A greedy manipulator, if you believe what Lyle Corrigan said. Before he died.

I studied Mark carefully. He'd arrived in Hawaiian-patterned swim trunks with a terry-cloth shirt trimmed in matching fabric and one of those little animal emblems that are supposed to indicate "expensive." Mark has Jack Kennedy-type hair that was not cut in Cedar Harbor, dark eyes and a ready smile. To be honest, in my previous encounters with him, I'd seen nothing to indicate he was anything except a shrewd businessman. Shrewd businessmen do not waste time, in my experience. He wanted something tonight. It wasn't difficult to guess what that was. Water.

Strange how water has been a source of discord almost since the inception of the United States. Certainly since the vast arid sections were settled. Times still aren't that different except that, presumably, differences are settled by negotiation now instead of guns. Or are they? I, for one, intended to keep a wary eye on Mark Gasper.

"I've been negligent," Al said, playing the genial host. "Let's all have a drink before we get down to business. No, no," he said to a rising Cyrus. "I'll get them. What'll you have?"

Once all that was settled, we leaned back in the steaming water with drinks in our hands. Not a good idea, I've heard, but my mostly lemony one surely wouldn't do any harm. I wasn't so sure about the drinks the others were having. At least, during all the confusion, I managed to place myself be-

tween Michael and Cyrus. I wanted to watch the faces of both
Al and Mark.

"Well, now," Al said, taking a sip. "As I was about to explain to these folks, I've asked you all here so that we can discuss Gasper Enterprises."

Surprise, surprise.

"And, of course, Shadybrook Meadows."

Ugh. The ultimate in misleading names.

"Let's have a toast to that worthy endeavor."

That was too much for any of us. Michael hesitated, glass
halfway to his mouth. Cyrus set his down firmly on the edge
of the tub. I, predictable, was the one to open my mouth.

"Oh, come on, Al."

"A bit premature," Mark soothed. "Although I hope I'll
have the backing of you people as we get the ball rolling again.
Shadybrook will be a development you'll all be proud of. I
hope you'll withhold judgment until you see my latest plans.
We've reserved large sections of greenbelt . . ."

He didn't have any choice, I knew, because of all the new
regulations regarding wetlands.

"And we've also set aside a section of beach with public
access . . ."

The section below the high bluff, no doubt. Wouldn't do
to have the public wandering in front of picture windows of
expensive homes.

"I don't see," Cyrus said, "why you're approaching us. I
understood the county was firm about the building moratorium."

"They were," Mark said, looking serious. "But the situation has changed."

Because Lyle Corrigan was no longer around to oppose
him?

"I think we've managed to address all their concerns, and

the good news is that I believe the moratorium is about to be lifted."

Good news? For whom?

Al watched the proceedings silently, a smug grin on his face. What was Al going to get out of this? I knew, suddenly, with certainty, that he *was* getting something tangible. Probably money.

I was pleased when Cyrus continued to be the spokesperson. I hate to always be the spoiler. "I think," he said, "that approaching our board is premature. When the lifting of the moratorium is official, well, then we can look at your plans." On my other side, Michael nodded vigorously.

"Of course," Mark said. "I wouldn't want it otherwise. Just thought it wise to bring you up to date." He downed his drink hastily. "I won't keep you people," he said. "I'm sure you have other business." He climbed from the hot tub and, after shaking Al's hand, departed.

Al's demeanor had changed by the time he turned around. A scowl was fixed on his forehead. "You people were rude to Mark," he said.

"Oh, now, Al," I said. "He's a businessman. Besides, what did you expect, dropping this on all of us unannounced?"

"I'm with Donna," Michael said. "The last I knew, we'd all agreed this development isn't a good idea for Cedar Harbor."

I glanced at him appreciatively. More than he usually says.

"Out of line, Al," Cyrus said. "Out of line. If the county removes the moratorium, that's time enough."

"Oh, all right," Al said, looking and sounding like a sulky child.

We discussed a few more small items, but no one's heart was in it. Besides, I felt like a stewed prune, and moved to sit on the edge of the tub. In a few minutes, I began to feel like a frozen stewed prune when the cooling breeze off the Sound changed to frigid.

"I'm going home," I announced, standing and pulling on my shirt.

"It's odd," said Cyrus as he stepped out of the tub, "how the county is changing its tune so quickly after Lyle's death."

"Just coincidence," Al said. "By the way, I hear that Lyle, Junior is coming home to take over the store."

"Oh, that's good," I said. "With Jolene missing and Marie incapacitated and all. I wonder why no one seems to know what's wrong with her."

Michael shrugged. "I don't think the doctors have decided. Marie's quite vehement about it, though."

We all turned to stare at him. He looked embarrassed. "I shouldn't have spoken, I guess. Please don't let it go any further. My wife's a medical technician, you know. She was in the room drawing blood, and she couldn't help hearing what Mrs. Corrigan was saying.

"She kept repeating, 'Someone poisoned me.' "

CHAPTER VII

Cyrus escorted me home from the Parrys'. His company was unavoidable unless I wanted to be impolite, since we said goodnight and walked out the front door at the same time. It was inevitable that we discuss the evening's events.

"You know Marie Corrigan," he said. "Is she an attention seeker?"

"No," I said firmly. "The exact opposite."

"The hysterical type?"

"I wouldn't have thought so, before Lyle died," I answered firmly. "But the day I went to her house . . ." I was remembering the look on Marie's face as she insisted that Jolene had become a liar. "I'm afraid that it's possible."

"What a strange family."

I nodded. "I'm sure most of the community never realized. I mean, successful businessman, wife who volunteers, children who never got into trouble. A perfect family, right? But as a teacher . . ." I was silent as I remembered the time Lyle, Junior had showed up with a bruised face. He could have injured it in an accident, of course, but he'd reacted in a peculiar manner when I asked what happened. He hung his head and mumbled something that I couldn't understand.

"Speak up, Lyle," I remember saying, a natural remark on my part.

"I—I just fell—fell down the stairs," he'd said then, not meeting my eyes.

That episode wasn't the only time he'd shown up with unusual injuries, I recalled with sudden clarity.

"What are you remembering this time?" Cyrus asked quietly. "I can always tell. You get that withdrawn expression, except for your eyes. They glow."

"Thanks a lot," I said. "Glowing eyes."

"My remark wasn't intended as an insult."

"No," I conceded, looking both ways before I stepped from the curb, "I don't suppose it was." Cyrus made a gesture as if he intended to take my arm, but I squelched that by pressing mine firmly against my side. Traffic along Beach Drive is much busier than it used to be. Busier, even, than last summer. There was a lot of new construction prior to the moratorium. We waited for a blue van coming in one direction and a yellow pickup from the other before crossing.

"Yes, I was remembering. How I wish we'd had the knowledge then, and the resources, so that I could have done something about my suspicions that his father hurt him. Funny how old memories are surfacing in my mind these days. The Corrigan children left town, and I hadn't thought of either of them until events forced them to my attention."

"Didn't you do anything regarding the poor kid?" Cyrus's voice was stern, and I was surprised. I would have thought that he might belong to the school that insists on blind obedience from offspring, with swift retribution to those who rebel.

"Do you have children?" I asked.

"I had one. He's dead."

Oh-oh. No wonder he spoke of grief. "I'm sorry," I said.

"I've adjusted."

I *was* sorry that I had inadvertently revived bad memories for Cyrus. I decided to return to our original topic of conversation. "Actually," I squinted as I concentrated, "I remember bringing the subject up with my principal."

My tone of voice must have given me away. "Who didn't believe you," Cyrus said.

"He played golf on Sundays with Lyle."

Cyrus grunted.

"We have to remember, though, that times *were* different. One rarely heard of child abuse. I'm sure it was there, perhaps even more prevalent—spanking was more accepted—but what happened at home was private and rarely discussed. The government certainly didn't take an interest."

We walked in silence for a moment more. Then he said, "What did you think about our friend, Al's, sudden turnaround concerning the Gasper development?"

"You mean, Shadybrook Meadows?"

Cyrus's moustache did the twitching that meant he was smiling underneath. "Exactly."

"I imagine I had the same reaction anyone else would. Al's on the take. What else?"

"What else, indeed? I just wanted to confirm that you agreed. What are we going to do about it?"

"At the very least, oppose Mark when we get the opportunity. Although, I have to admit to mixed feelings. He was planning affordable housing for part of the development, and we all know how that's needed. At least, those of us with social consciousness do." I glanced sideways at him, but he didn't respond. I really knew nothing about Cyrus's political attitudes. Conservative, no doubt, but then I have been wrong before. Not often, but once in a while.

"I just don't want to be a party to anything nefarious," I went on. "Or, I should say, I don't think Al should get by with whatever he's up to. He doesn't need money, obviously. What's gotten into him?"

"Greed isn't restricted to the poor."

I snorted. "*That* has certainly been obvious in recent years, with the scandals on Wall Street."

"I think," Cyrus said, "that I'll do a little snooping and see what I can find out. Has the same thing been happening in the county? Is that why the moratorium is going to be lifted, if, in fact, it is?"

"It won't be easy."

He touched his moustache. I do believe he was twirling it. I looked at him appraisingly. Cyrus, it was obvious, was looking forward to playing detective.

"More challenge that way," he said.

A sudden thought occurred to me. "By the way, weren't you supposed to take notes of the meeting?"

"I have a pad and pen in my pocket, but hot tubs and minutes didn't seem compatible. It won't be hard to reconstruct."

He might do a better job that way, it occurred to me, than when he was trying to take part actively in a meeting and record it at the same time. We'd arrived in front of his place. He indicated his intent to escort me to my own door, but I squelched that, too. "I'm capable of moving another twenty-five feet by myself, Cyrus," I said, "but thanks, anyway."

He shrugged and said, "You're welcome," but the expression on his face didn't match the ritual answer. He looked decidedly annoyed. Did he think me discourteous?

Carrie Sanderson seemed to have put her animosity on hold in order to hear what Noreen Parry was saying. Neither noticed me as they came out the post office door and strolled up the street. I heard snatches, though, and they were talking about Marie and the poison. Clearly, the word had gotten out. Or, perhaps, Noreen was in the process of disseminating the information acquired last night from Michael.

As I continued on inside the post office, I could see others deep in conversation, and they were all, it appeared, discussing the subject. The Corrigans in general and Marie in particular. Especially, the fact that she'd been poisoned.

"Donna," a voice called behind me.

I turned to see Sue Reilly, struggling to bring her two sons through the door in their stroller.

"Hi," I answered. "Just a sec." I reached back and propped the door so she could maneuver inside.

"Have you heard?" she asked as soon as she caught her breath. "Marie Corrigan was poisoned, that's why they took her to the hospital."

"Are they sure?" I asked. "And, who did . . ."

"Who, they don't know. Jake was willing to tell me that much. When I bumped into him just a minute ago, over at the bakery," she added.

"Uh-huh," I said with a straight face.

She glanced at me sharply, but went on. "The word is, they're sure she was poisoned but they don't know what with. Not something ordinary, like arsenic or strychnine."

"What a world we've come to, when arsenic and strychnine are considered ordinary," I commented.

"Well, you know what I mean. It wasn't something someone picked up at the hardware store for rats or whatever."

"How is she doing?" I asked.

"Fine, I guess. I mean, she'll live."

"That's good news. I hear that Lyle, Junior has come back to help out at the hardware store," I added. "But, that's right, you wouldn't have known him."

"No, I don't. But I'm glad for Marie's sake. Stop that!" She was speaking to Todd who was pounding Jeff's head. "Oh, Lord, they've been like this all morning. I'd better pick up my mail and get home."

We said goodbye, and I went on to my own box around the corner from Sue's. A bank statement, an insurance bill and a mailing from the Retired Teachers. I wasn't going to make the mistake of going to their gathering this year. Who knew what would happen in my absence this time?

When I came out, I glanced over at the hardware store. Now might be a good time to study their tile selection, in case I went ahead with plans to remodel the bath.

I smiled at the clerk who usually waited on me as I passed by the plumbing section. "Hi, Mrs. Galbreath," he said. Such an agreeable young man. I really should find out what *his* name was one of these days. Paint and tile were housed in a separate room at the rear, and I headed in that direction, past the desk where one paid for purchases.

"Mrs. Galbreath?"

A voice sounded behind me. I turned, and saw a tall young man—young by my standards, maybe forty.

"It really *is* you," he said, rounding a display of roofing tar and extending his hand. "Lyle, Junior, here, although I've gone by my middle name of Will since I left town."

"How nice to see you." I let him take my hand, which he pumped vigorously as I studied him. Yes, I could see the youngster who'd been in my sixth-grade class. Oh, of course I'd run into him around town after that, but the age when a teacher relates to a child on a day-to-day basis is what sticks in one's mind. He'd grown into a man quite a bit taller than his father, certainly slimmer, and quite good-looking, even if his dark hair had receded considerably. I saw all this in an instant, of course.

"I'd have known you anywhere," he said, "even if I hadn't heard Peter speak to you."

Ah, Peter. I'd remember that. "What a nice thing to say," I responded.

"But true. A person never forgets his favorite teacher. You're the one . . ." He hesitated as he thought. "You're the one who taught me to think."

"That's absolutely the nicest thing anyone has ever said about my teaching. I'm sorry," I continued, "about all the distress in your family. Your father's death and all. How is your mother doing?"

"Very well, thank you. She's home now. Why don't you stop by? I know she'd be glad to see you."

"I'll try," I said, knowing full well that it was unlikely that Marie would be glad to see me. But there was no point in telling Lyle—Will, I must remember to call him that—what had occurred between his mother and me. He was likely to hear the whole story when she recovered. He might not be quite so cordial the next time he saw me.

"Can I offer you assistance?"

"No thanks. Today I'm just browsing. I wanted to look at your tile selection."

"Right back here." He gestured. "Let me know if I can help." He turned back toward the counter, where two customers chatted as they waited to be served.

I went on to the tile display, but my heart wasn't in it. Finally, I admitted to myself that it hadn't been tile at all that had brought me into the store, but curiosity. I'd satisfied that, so I might as well leave. I waved at Will as I departed.

It was lunchtime when I reached home, so I toasted some bread and slathered it with jam. Not the healthiest lunch, but one that appealed to me. In the interest of vitamins, I topped it off with a peach. The ripe-looking fruit wasn't satisfying since it clearly had been picked at some distant orchard and not tree-ripened. I lay down on my bed as usual, but sleep eluded me, so I decided I might as well put my time to use and get to work in the garden.

By three-thirty, I'd accomplished a gratifying amount. My compost pile had expanded and my wheelbarrow was full of weeds that might have spread in an obnoxious manner. These I'd squash into the garbage can. My collecting container was full of slugs.

"Glad to see you're not watering."

I jumped a mile. Cyrus had somehow sneaked in behind me. "How did you get in here without my hearing?" I asked, after I regained my composure.

"Simple. I WD-40'd your gate the other day. That was all it took to stop the squeaking, as I told you. You didn't notice?"

I sighed loudly as I shoved the slug carton under a fern frond. "No, I didn't notice." Perhaps I should have thanked him, but I'd been perfectly satisfied with my gate the way it was. No one ever sneaked up on me. I stood, slowly stretching my back to get the creaks out.

"Looks like you need a chiropractor," he said. "I can recommend a good one."

I declined. No chiropractor could fix what was caused by a combination of aging and hard work.

"I didn't mean to startle you," Cyrus went on. "Just stopped by to tell you that I'm getting a pet."

"You are?" I asked. "Let me guess. A boxer."

Cyrus looked pained.

"No, a bulldog. Or could it be a pit bull?"

"You have a peculiar picture of my likes and dislikes," he said. "As a matter of fact, I brought her to introduce." He reached into a shopping bag that I hadn't noticed and pulled forth a pure white kitten.

The look on his face was priceless—gentle, adoring. I could have easily laughed, but I was glad I managed to restrain myself by stroking the kitten. So soft. It meowed in response with a surprisingly loud noise. "It's precious," I said. "Have you picked a name?"

"Indeed. Meet Donna Two."

"You've got to be kidding." I ran my fingers through my hair, no doubt making it stand up in an un-kitten-like manner. "What will the neighbors think when you bellow in your inimitable manner for her to come in? And, why?"

"My dear Donna, since when has either of us cared what the neighbors think? And, to answer your second question, because she reminded me of you."

"Me?" I squeaked. Surely not. Dainty, even pretty.

He nodded. "Loud and with a mind of her own. Just thought I should let you know she belongs to me in case she becomes lost or something. With my fenced yard, though, she should stay home."

"Don't bet on it. Cats like to roam, and no fence can stop a determined one. I used to have cats, but when the last died, I vowed not to tie myself down with another."

"I've never had one before," he said, setting her down on the ground. "Nor a dog, either."

How sad. No wonder his emotional development had been stunted. Well, there was nothing like a pet to help one in that area.

"You heard that the diagnosis of Marie's illness had been confirmed?" he asked.

I nodded. "I stopped at the hardware store to see Lyle, Junior, and he said she's home."

"Still no trace of his sister, I take it?"

"Apparently not. At least, no one was talking about it at the post office. Sue Reilly would have told me. She seems to have an inside track with Jake these days."

"Hmm," he said, rubbing his chin and watching the kitten chase a butterfly, one of nature's more charming moments.

They never catch them, of course, which renders the act harmless and pleasing. "Makes one wonder what the results would have been had you only recognized that young woman sooner."

What an annoying remark. "Cyrus," I said, "half of the people in town had known her as a young woman. You might say I was remarkably astute to spot that Karen and Jolene were one and the same."

He almost sneered. Not quite. Cyrus doesn't show disdain that broadly. "I remember every man I ever served with, and that covers a period at least as long as your teaching career," he said.

"Well, bully for you," I retorted. "You weren't dealing with them as twelve-year-olds. Sit down," I said on sudden impulse. "I'll show you. I have pictures of all the classes I taught. I'll show you how much she'd changed."

"That's not necessary," he said.

"Oh, yes it is, if you're going to goad me like that. *Sit down*," I ordered. I didn't wait to see if he did.

It took me longer than I'd have liked to locate the proper box. I'm organized in a disorganized manner. I finally located the right one, a brown carton on the top shelf of my closet. I removed the stack of photos, which represented the sum total of my teaching, and carried them out into the back yard.

"Here," I said, pulling a chair up beside Cyrus. "Just a minute, while I locate the right year. Let's see . . ." I leafed through the pile. Some day I should put them into an album.

"Here it is." I laid the picture on the table and studied it. What memories it brought back. The tall girl in the back row was now a surgeon, I'd heard, and the smaller boy in front of her was in jail. I moved my finger along until I located Jolene, sitting on the ground in the front row. "There she is," I said, pointing, as Cyrus leaned forward to look. "See?"

75

Jolene didn't exactly stare back as most of the children appeared to do. She hadn't been looking at the camera. Instead, as I had remembered was her habit, the skinny, small girl held her head low so that her dirt-colored hair hid much of her face. No resemblance at all to the Karen we had met recently. Part of it was manner, and of course that didn't show entirely in the picture. Somewhere, somehow, Jolene had acquired a little gumption in recent years, had learned to stand up straight.

"Now tell me you would have recognized that child as the grown-up Karen."

He peered at the picture, finally bringing a pair of glasses out of his pocket to study it more closely. "Hmm."

"Well?" I prodded.

"You're right." The admission was grudging.

I had begun to smile triumphantly when I noticed something else in the picture. "Give me that," I said, snatching it away.

He eyed me with a question in his eyes.

"Oh my God," I said.

"What? What?"

"See that girl?" I pointed to the equally shy-appearing student seated next to Jolene. "How could I have forgotten?"

"*What,*" he demanded, yet again.

"That's Mary Larson," I said. "Gloria's daughter. I had forgotten that Mary was in the same class with Jolene. They were, in fact, friends."

"So?"

"She killed herself that year."

"How distressing, and . . . how odd," Cyrus said.

CHAPTER VIII

We stared at the picture silently, both engrossed in our own thoughts, until the kitten's bid for attention snapped us back to the present. With her head swiveling to show that she didn't care which of us gave her her due, Donna Two, sitting between us, emitted complaining meows. Loud. Just as Cyrus had said. I sighed and picked her up. Satisfied, she kneaded my thigh, then settled down with a purr that was only a few decibels lower than her previous clamor. Poor thing. Maybe some of us need to be loud to achieve what we want in this world, particularly if we're female.

Absentmindedly, Cyrus reached over and scratched her ears. "It can't have anything to do with the situation," he said. "I mean, Jolene's friendship with—what did you say her name was? Gloria's daughter?"

"Mary."

He nodded. "Mary. Poor girl. Did anyone ever find out why she did such a thing?"

"Not really. They only knew that she was a lonely, unhappy girl. She'd never had any friends at all, evidently, until she and Jolene drifted together. Misfits. Leftovers. What remained after the rest of the class divided into friendships and cliques. She left a note, as I recall, but it lacked specifics."

"Was there a Mister Larson?"

"Yes, but he was a distant sort of man who no one knew well. I have never decided whether Mary was strange—and I can't help categorizing her that way—because her father was antisocial and apparently uncaring or because her mother was so domineering."

"What happened to him?"

"He died a few years later. He seemed to—to just shrink after her death, and finally he withered completely away. I guess the image he projected of being uncaring was untrue. A tragedy affects everyone around it. I know suicides are sometimes seen as a form of revenge, but it's difficult to imagine a twelve-year-old having that sort of motive."

"Of course not. She wasn't old enough to hate."

From the look on Cyrus's face, he'd been involved with hate. As the recipient? Or the giver?

"How long ago was this?" he asked, picking up the school picture and staring at it again.

"Umm," I said, "maybe twenty, twenty-one . . ." I leaned forward and took the picture from his hand. "It's on the back. So, it was twenty-three years ago this winter."

"Well, as sad as it was, I can't see that a girl's death twenty-three years ago could have anything to do with the Corrigan woman's disappearance now."

"Or Lyle's murder. I know. It just struck me, looking at that picture, what a coincidence it was that tragedy should strike both girls. Things happen that way in life, though. Some people would say it was an evil star or something, but undoubtedly it was the fact that two girls whose very natures set them up for unhappiness tended naturally to gravitate together. I wonder, though . . ." A thought suddenly came to me. "Wouldn't you think it would have been natural for Gloria Larson to recognize Jolene before I did?"

"Yes. I would."

"I think I'll nail her on it. Although, of course, none of this really is my business."

He waggled his eyebrows the way he does. "You might say that." That glint that I'd decided might be humor, after all, flashed in his eyes.

Did he actually mean he thought I was intruding where I should not? I couldn't decide.

I looked at the calendar. Was it really a month since the last Historical Society meeting? The one where Gloria had insulted me as I cowered in the restroom stall? Well, I wouldn't let her drive me away from the organization. This meeting promised to be more interesting than usual. They'd snared an anthropologist from the U who'd just published a book on the Northwest Indians. I wanted to hear him.

One of the benefits of being in a drought period in the Puget Sound country was the continuing sunshine. Although, now that it was July, we normally expect the best weather of the year. It was too nice out to be cooped up any longer than necessary, though, so I decided to walk to the meeting even though I had promised to provide flowers for the table. I worked in the garden in the morning, then just before lunch picked some nice white fluffy daisies—I'd been given the plant by a friend, so I was never sure what they were, but probably Esther Reed—and some blue spiked veronica. For color I added a butter-yellow yarrow. I then changed into a cotton rose-and-white striped shirt and blue pants, and then, for comfort, put on my athletic shoes. When I was ready, I set out.

It is sad to see brown lawns in this normally verdant area, but people are adapting. The Rodenbergs down the street recently hired a landscaping firm to replace their front grass with non-thirsty perennials and artfully arranged rocks. Well done, as adequate as lawn, I noted as I passed, but somehow in my mind not as handsome as the old standbys. Who could do without roses and peonies and lilies of the valley? Even the so-called native rhododendrons need water. I, myself, am switching to drought-resistant plants whenever possible, but I'm not willing to give up the hobby I'd dreamed of having time to really pursue when I retired.

I'd dallied a little too long inspecting yards, I could see as I approached the library. People were beginning to gather. Just as I had always told the Historical Society, providing interesting programs is the key to increased participation. I hurried inside.

A harried Carrie Sanderson greeted me at the door and snatched the flowers. "I was beginning to wonder if something had happened to you," she said. "You're never late."

I started to apologize, but just then a voice behind me said, "I offered to bring the flowers." Gloria Larson, who else.

Gritting my teeth, I glanced at my watch before saying, "I'm not late. Not really. People are arriving early. I'll help you, Carrie," I offered.

"Oh, we're ready and you're entirely right, Donna. I just get nervous about these things, especially when strangers are coming. Do you think we'll have enough cookies?"

I glanced at the table which threatened to sag under the homemade goodies produced by our members. "There's plenty," I assured her. With a peek to ascertain that Gloria was no longer in earshot, I apologized. "I *am* sorry I wasn't here earlier."

"No problem," she said as she arranged the flowers in the cut-glass vase we keep at the library for these occasions. "There. What do you think?"

"Perfect," I said.

She smiled happily. "They couldn't be otherwise, when

you bring them." With a surreptitious look around, she whispered, "I always feel Gloria's bouquets are so—so flamboyant."

My thoughts exactly. Feeling satisfied, I turned to see who had come.

The speaker had attracted more men than usual, mostly retirees, of course, since it was a daytime meeting. Standing in one corner talking to Sue was Cyrus. What do you know? He'd never shown the least interest in our activities before. He was dressed in gray slacks and a blue blazer. Tie, of course, though he was one of the few men in the room who wore one. As usual, he was pressed, trimmed and immaculate. I glanced down at my own attire. Cyrus wouldn't approve of the appearance of my shoes. There wasn't anything I could do about them. The glowing white athletic shoes foisted on women these days always turn a dirty gray after wear.

I'd have walked over to speak with Sue, but I didn't feel like coping with Cyrus at the moment.

A flurry near the door made me glance in that direction. To my surprise, Marie Corrigan came in, followed by her son, who held one hand protectively against her back. I'd bet her participation was his doing. He'd seemed the sort to urge his mother into society again for her own good. I agreed with him, of course. I decided to do what I could and greet her.

I had to stand in line, but finally I was pressing her hand with mine and saying, "Marie, so good to see you. I hope you're feeling better?"

"Much." Her smile appeared forced as her gaze flicked across my face, not really focusing on me.

Oh, boy. I didn't blame her. Perhaps I should have stayed on the other side of the room. But our meeting was inevitable, eventually. Perhaps another apology? But how does one really atone for being a factor in the disappearance of a daughter? Her eyes shifted toward the next greeter.

Impulsively, I said, "I—I *am* sorry. For what I . . ."

Now she squeezed *my* hand and did look directly at me. "Don't apologize," she whispered. "You were right in your actions. I know that." This time her smile looked genuine and I felt greatly comforted. What a truly nice person she was, and so sad that she had been burdened with Lyle for a husband for so many years.

As usual, we had a business meeting before the speaker was introduced, mercifully short this time. When Gloria waved her hand for attention, I groaned inwardly.

Carrie gave her the floor. "As program chairman," Gloria began, and I wondered when she was going to learn not to use that sexist title, "I'd like to thank everyone who helped in to-day's preparations." She droned on, with thanks to practi-cally everyone in the club for something. I was surprised that she didn't praise the library cleaning staff.

"And all you ladies who baked your favorite cookie rec-ipes," she went on, "and especially to our renowned gar-dener, Donna Galbreath, for the stunning floral display which so demonstrates her talents."

I snapped to attention. Well . . . Perhaps I'd been mean-spirited in agreeing with Carrie that Gloria's bouquets were flamboyant. Colorful might be a better word. I ventured a smile of thanks in Gloria's direction. A strange expression of satisfaction flitted across her face. Maybe because she'd de-cided to say something nice to make up for her remarks of the previous month. Someone surely had told her that she'd been overheard.

Finally we got down to the nitty-gritty of the speaker. Dr. Cavanaugh, a younger man than I expected, considering his renown, was as interesting as I had hoped. He had many tales of the collecting of the magnificent art of the Northwest Coast Indians, some of which had not been done in the spirit of helping the native people.

"And so," he concluded, "don't forget the special exhibit coming up this fall at the Burke Museum."

He received a nice round of applause, and then the crowd surged either toward the refreshment table or the one set up by the local bookstore to hold Dr. Cavanaugh's books. I, too, stood in the line there and purchased his latest. He graciously scribbled an incomprehensible autograph.

I took the book, and turned. Perhaps I could join Sue now for a moment. I scanned the crowd, looking for her. I must have done an obvious double-take when I spotted her— seated and talking animatedly with Mark Gasper. He was hanging on her every word. Hmph.

I then noticed Gloria Larson standing not far away. Nerved by her unexpected tribute to my flowers, I decided to approach her concerning her daughter Mary's friendship with Jolene. A touchy subject, but surely the intervening years made it possible for her to talk about Mary.

"Gloria," I said as she broke away from the group she'd been speaking with, "I've been doing a lot of thinking lately about the past, even going over old school pictures. The other day I—ran across the one of your daughter Mary's class." Had my hesitation been noticeable? "Such an unhappy event," I finished. Did I imagine a slight stiffening in her demeanor?

"Yes, it was," she said sadly. "Mary would be turning thirty-six at Christmas time, if she were alive. It doesn't seem possible so many years have passed."

"I know," I agreed, thinking how difficult it was to believe that I could be of retirement age, even if I had retired a bit early.

"I was surprised," I went on, "when I saw the picture with Mary and Jolene Corrigan sitting together in the front row. I'd forgotten that they'd become friends. I remember hoping at the time that the friendship would make Mary—happier."

"So did I," she said softly.

"It's odd how looking at those pictures brings back memories long forgotten. Gloria," I ventured, "didn't you recognize Jolene when she came back as Karen? Didn't she at least come and see you?"

"No, she didn't and I didn't. Donna, I still find the subject of Mary painful. Do you mind?"

"Of course not," I said. I felt guilty yet again. I was doing a lot of that lately. The loss of a child must truly be one of nature's most difficult events. "I'm sorry."

"I try to remember her as a small girl," she said, "a happy toddler. That's the way I think of her in Heaven."

I nodded.

"She never was difficult, played so contentedly by herself. I remember her favorite stuffed animal, a teddy bear named Sammy. She sat and rocked him by the hour."

I nodded again, feeling like a wound-up toy. What was there to say? It sounded, though, as if the roots of Mary's loneliness had already been probing deep.

"She'd sing little songs . . ." Gloria's eyes clearly weren't seeing me, but rather those long ago days with her daughter. I felt like a heel to have started this. I glanced around, hoping for an interruption. I was relieved to see Cyrus heading in our direction. I gestured quickly for him to come over, hoping Gloria wouldn't notice.

"Good afternoon, Donna, Mrs. Larson," he said.

She shook her head as if to clear it, but didn't answer immediately.

"I'm not sure we've been introduced. I'm Cyrus Bates, Donna's neighbor." He held out a hand.

Her expression changed from soft with memories to her usual hard mask as she pulled herself together. Then after the typical inanities expressed by two people who don't know each other and don't really care, she said, "I think I'll have another cup of coffee. Nice to meet you, Mr. Bates. Excuse me."

She headed toward the refreshment table.

I exhaled in relief. "I was glad to see you," I said.

"A first?" That eyebrow lifted to new heights.

I didn't deign to answer.

"I thought you looked like you needed rescuing," he said.

"I did. I confronted her about not recognizing Jolene, Cyrus, and she evaded me by saying she didn't want to talk about her daughter. And then she proceeded to do just that. Not about a meaningful age, though, just about Mary as a toddler."

"Nothing ventured, nothing gained."

"I feel sorry for her. I guess I've said it before, but perhaps she wouldn't have become so difficult if Mary had lived."

"Perhaps. But it's my experience that people's characteristics are only accentuated in difficult times. The good become better and the bad . . ." He didn't finish the thought, instead changed the subject. "Have you had refreshments yet?"

"No, I haven't, and I'd love some, now that the crowd has thinned," I said. We moved over to the table. Carrie presided over the tea at one end and Jill Tanger the coffee at the other. Carrie handed me a filled cup, and I browsed over the goodies. "Oh, someone contributed those wonderful lemon crisp cookies again," I said. "My very favorite. I've been meaning to find out who makes them and ask for the recipe. Do you know who brought them, Carrie?"

She shook her head. "We could inquire at a meeting sometime, though."

"I'd appreciate that."

Cyrus was at the other end of the table, getting a refill of his coffee. Behind me, I noticed that Marie and her son were still here, speaking with a group of the Historical Society regulars, including Noreen Parry, who always takes a break from The Drugstore to attend our meetings. As I turned toward them, Bessie Amherst, one of our older members and one of the founders of the group, laid a pudgy hand on Marie's wrist before she spoke. "But my dear," she asked, "have they not determined with what you were poisoned?"

"As a matter of fact," Will answered for her, "we just heard the results this morning. We'd never have found out, evidently, if it hadn't been for that new young internist at the hospital, Dr. Chung. He was particularly persistent. The lab people now say that it was most likely one of the monobasic alkaloids such as aconitine. Comes from a plant called monkshood. It's a relatively common perennial, and most any avid gardener would know about its poisonous qualities."

Cyrus moved alongside me. He'd heard Will, too, as had all nearby.

"Cyrus," I whispered out of the side of my mouth, "why is everyone staring at me?"

CHAPTER IX

"I keep telling you, they weren't looking at you." Cyrus apparently meant to reassure me, but it wasn't working.

I had found no graceful way to prevent him from walking home with me. Truth to tell, his support after the distasteful moment was welcome. At least he didn't seem to assume I was a poisoner just because I happened to be the person in the community best known as a gardener.

"Monkshood," he said musingly. "Never heard of it. Don't suppose you have one."

"Well . . ."

"You have one."

"Almost anyone with a garden as extensive as mine does. Nice plant. It comes in yellow as well as the more common blue. But Cyrus, owning the plant doesn't make me an attempted murderer."

"Did you know it was poisonous?"

"Um, yes, I guess. I do believe I recall a reference to that in *Sunset*. But a lot of plants are, I understand. I never studied the question. I'm not planning to eat any of them."

We walked along silently for a moment. I didn't know what he was thinking about, but my mind was filled with unpleasant images.

I guess he did have an inkling as to where my thoughts were leading, though, because he said, pointing to both sides, "There are lots of other gardeners in Cedar Harbor.

All you have to do is look at all these yards to see that."

I watched a man mowing a lawn as we approached the next block. "Hailey's Landscape Service," said the sign on the side of his truck. "Cyrus," I explained, "there are pleasantly done yards, taken care of by someone else . . ." I gestured toward the truck. "And there are those maintained by people who are focused narrowly and wouldn't know the difference between a verbena and a veronica, such as you, I might point out."

He shrugged. "I'd know where to find out if I wanted to."

"Perhaps, but using a plant as poison probably wouldn't occur to you," I said.

"No, I'd probably take a more direct approach. Don't they say poison is a woman's weapon?"

"I've heard that, but I never quite believed it."

"Nevertheless, there have to be a few other people here who are knowledgeable about plants. Haven't I read about some garden club?"

I snorted. "Our local one's prime purpose is to have lunch and socialize and tour other people's creations. If they'd just stay home and use the time to work on their own instead . . . But you're right, of course, there are others, and I suppose when people have time to think about it, they'll realize that. Although somehow I've been more intimately involved with the subject than anyone else who comes to mind."

I thought for a moment as we continued toward our respective homes. "There's Serena Cantrell, over on Blackberry Road, who specializes in native plants, and there's George Hatchen, out in The Heights, who grows little else but old roses, and there's—Gloria Larson. GLORIA LARSON," I shrieked. "That *witch!* She wasn't being nice today, she was pointing the finger at me and away from her! She must have already heard the report about the poison. I *knew it!* I knew there was something peculiar going on in that thing that she probably considers a mind. Just when I was feeling sorry for her, too!"

A muffled snort made me glance at Cyrus in surprise. He doesn't normally vent uncouth noises. As I looked at him, he chuckled. Then a guffaw bent him over. He actually slapped his thigh. I didn't know people really did that. I stopped walking, put my hands on my hips and glared.

Finally he noticed me. "I'm sorry," he apologized. "I couldn't help it. You're right, of course. But you'd better . . ." He couldn't quite wipe the smile from his face. "You'd better quit underestimating that woman's mental acuity."

"I've never seen you laugh before, Cyrus," I said.

"Not an awful lot to laugh at in this world, is there?" He pulled a handkerchief from his pocket and wiped his eyes. A carefully folded, perfectly white handkerchief, of course. That's Cyrus. Always prepared. He had to have been a Boy Scout.

"Normally I find plenty to laugh at." I knew my voice sounded huffy.

"Come on," he said, taking my arm. "As the kids say, 'lighten up.' "

I shook his hand away. "You wouldn't feel that way if everyone looked at *you* when the discussion turned toward murder."

"They weren't looking at you."

How I wished Roberta lived close by, as she had for so many years. She didn't marry until her early thirties, at which time she moved to New York because Joel's work was there. *I* had resented her giving up a perfectly good job of her own here, but she insisted that she didn't mind.

She has such a practical outlook on life's little matters, and we're always able to share our worries with each other.

Cyrus might be willing to accept that I was unlikely to be a poisoner, but to keep insisting that I wasn't the object of everyone's attention and surmising at the meeting . . . ? Bull. He was obtuse and unobserving *or* he was just trying to make me feel better. Would Cyrus do that? No, I decided. Not him. He had clearly demonstrated his unawareness of my feelings in his past dealings with me, so why should I expect otherwise now?

Roberta would undoubtedly try to make me feel better, but in a logical manner. I could just hear her. "Mother," she'd say, "they probably *were* looking at you. Everyone knows you're the expert. Maybe they thought you could tell them something about the poison."

I couldn't, I realized. As I'd told Cyrus, I'd vaguely known that many of the plants I dealt with could be poisonous if ingested, but that had always seemed immaterial. Since I'd never planned to murder anyone nor even to sample plants as food, I hadn't paid attention. I'd have to look in the library for a book on the subject.

But Roberta . . . I blinked. Thinking of my daughter made me realize two things. I hadn't checked my mail today, and it really had been longer than usual since I'd heard from her. I glanced at the clock. It was just after five. I'd give her a call.

There was no answer. When the answering machine kicked on, I left a message. "Just wanted to talk," I said. "Call me when you have a chance."

I watched the news on TV. The usual mayhem. The weatherman said a low was moving in and we might actually have rain before morning. What a relief that would be. Come to think of it, the sky had been changing even as I walked home from the library with Cyrus, but I'd been too upset to really pay attention. The crisp blue of the morning had been replaced by streaky clouds. I turned off the TV and checked my own barometer. The weatherman was right. The pressure had dropped considerably during the day.

I expected the ring of the phone all evening, but it was unusually silent. Roberta and Joel must have gone out for the evening, perhaps to a play. That was one of the reasons Roberta enjoyed New York, she always said. Well, in the morning I'd no doubt find a long letter waiting in my post office box.

Often I'd have a call from someone else during the hours after dinner. I suppose, I thought bitterly, they're all talking to each other about monkshood and Marie and no one has the nerve to call me.

During the night, the wind rose as predicted. I heard a few thuds on the roof as well as the howling in my screens. There'd be work to do in the morning. Finally, the wind died down and the rain started with a sudden burst that made me smile sleepily. Good. The plants would love it. So would the slugs, a quiet voice said to me as I was almost asleep. Nothing's perfect, I told the voice, and became immediately unconscious.

That's not to say that I didn't have wild dreams. I did, but they were ones that were difficult to remember in their entirety come morning. Nightmares, actually. I know that Lyle flitted through, and Al, emitting gracious desire to get his own way. And Gloria. Always Gloria. I think slugs were in there, too, although I'm not sure where. Maybe I was transporting my crop to *her* garden.

What a delicious idea. I sat up in bed with a smile, ready to get to work. Not on depositing my gastropods in her yard. That wouldn't be really practical. Somehow the revenge, though, even if only in my mind, gave me a lift. Why did I spend the night dreaming about unpleasant people? There are so many amiable ones, Carrie, Sue for example. Cyrus had been strangely absent from my nighttime unpleasantries. Well, as villains went, he wasn't on a par with the rest, I supposed.

Lifting the shade in my bedroom and peering out at the rain-soaked landscape, I saw that the yard looked just as I had expected. Branches littered the grass and plants drooped, some of them snapped off. The roses wouldn't have liked the weather. I dressed in my work clothes and ate breakfast quickly. I don't really mind cleanup after a storm, which is part of nature, after all. I look on the work as a toll paid for the rain received. There had been enough this time to soak the ground thoroughly, I could see as soon as I got outside.

There was a damp feel to the air, bordering on a drizzle, and the sky was still overcast. It would burn off, though, and give us a delightful afternoon. Typical Puget Sound weather in the summer, so much more so than the heat we'd been having. I gathered branches first, bundling the larger for the next yard pickup we'd have, then tackling the smaller. Most of them would be all right in the compost, along with the broken bachelor's buttons and daisies.

I gathered slugs as I went. They always come out of their hiding places when it's damp. I'm not sure where they all go. Of course, one encounters them when turning over a loose board or a rock, but I try to keep such tempting places to a minimum. They burrow in the ground or something, or so many wouldn't show up when conditions are right for them.

"I thought I might find you back here."

I jumped, then turned to see Jake Santorini with his hand on the open gate. "Oh!" I said. "I *wish* Cyrus hadn't oiled that thing. You startled me."

"Sorry," he said. "Can I come in?"

"Of course." I stood, brushing the knees of my old jeans, although I didn't know why. Jake hadn't come to inspect my clothes. What Jake *might* have come for made me nervous. "What can I do for you?" I asked.

"Just answer a couple of questions. I . . ."

"Officer Santorini," I interrupted, "surely you have enough sense not to think I poisoned Marie Corrigan just because I supposedly know more about plants than anyone else around here?"

He grinned, looking younger and more pleasant than he'd first appeared. "Yeah," he said, "*I* do."

"And who . . . ? Let me guess. Our esteemed Chief of Police sent you."

"Well . . . yeah," he admitted. "But I thought it was a good idea because . . ."

"Hasn't it occurred to anyone that I would have had to have a reason? Not many people go around poisoning others, not to mention shooting them, just for fun."

"As I was going to say, I thought talking to you was a good idea because you know plants so well, an expert witness, so to speak."

I grumbled a little under my breath. "Does that mean I'm forgiven for my earlier . . . transgression?"

"I guess," he said. "If you promise not to do it again."

He sounded like a teacher or a parent. Chief Donniker would have loved it. I wondered why he hadn't come himself. It must not have occurred to him that he'd have an opportunity to humiliate me in person or he'd have been right there in my backyard instead of Jake, leaning against the trunk of my Douglas fir.

"I *am* sorry," I said. "It was a serious mistake in judgment. No, I won't do it again."

"What I wanted to know . . . tell me about monkshood."

"Well, it's a perennial, in the buttercup or crowfoot family if I remember correctly. Looks rather like a larkspur, if you're familiar with them. One native variety, if I'm not mistaken, grows all the way from Arizona to Canada. Obviously, it's not that unusual a plant. Called wolfsbane sometimes, too. If you want to know about its toxic properties, though, I can't really give you a lot of information. I vaguely knew it was poisonous, but I can't tell you if it's the flower or the leaves or . . . Come to think of it, I don't believe they were in bloom when Marie was attacked. Do you know what she had eaten?" I asked.

With a wry grin, he said, "Right down to the last olive."

That was one procedure I didn't think I wanted to know about. The results, yes. I'm a naturally curious person, I admit that, but there are limits. "It occurs to me that it must have been a slow-acting poison, if she didn't get sick until the next day."

He shook his head. "Nope. No way. Extremely fast acting. She ate an early lunch, because she had plans for later in the day. That fact that it hit her so quickly was a clue to the poison, I understand. She was lucky to be able to reach the phone."

"How did she . . . I mean, what was the poison in?"

"Lasagna. What we don't know, unfortunately, is where it came from. People had brought food by the truckload after Lyle was shot, and Marie had no idea where this particular contribution came from. The poisoner would have made sure of that. The lasagna was in a throw-away aluminum container; we were able to retrieve it from the garbage. She didn't even know when it had arrived, since she put everything that she could into her freezer immediately. So—no leads there."

"I see. Well, I'm sorry, Jake. I really am. Poisonous plants are not a subject I've ever boned up on. I'm sure there are experts . . . ?"

"Of course. The thought even . . . well, it occurred to

Chief Donniker. What I thought you might help me with, is suggestions. Who you know around here that you'd consider an expert. That sort of thing."

"An expert on poisons or plants?"

For a second I thought of naming Gloria Larson, and I'm ashamed to say I had a moment of glee in thinking of how I was in a position to make things uncomfortable for her. But, no. My better instincts prevailed.

I mentally ran down the list of the other gardeners I knew, including all those in the local club. No one had any particular connection with the Corrigans, and I saw no reason to inflict the police on any of them. Attacking the question from the other direction, who on my own list of suspicious characters—Al Parry, Mark Gasper, and even, although I hated to place her there, Carrie Sanderson—was a gardener? Not one of them to my knowledge.

"I can't help you," I said. "Anyone could do research on the subject and could find monkshood here and there, in a nursery if nowhere else. Why don't you suggest to the Chief that he look for a motive instead of who might have the knowledge?"

Jake smiled, and the expression now wasn't nearly as pleasant. "I can't speak for my boss, but believe it or not, Mrs. Galbreath, the thought had occurred to me." He shut his notebook with a snap. "If anything occurs to you, anything at all, concerning the people involved, I'd appreciate it if you'd give me a call. I'm sure you are as interested in finding the murderer as anyone."

"Of course," I said. "I truly am and will." I had the impression that I had irritated Jake, and I certainly hadn't meant to do that. I simply wanted to be sure of facts before I gave him names. I don't believe in vague accusations.

He left through the gate, and I glanced at my watch. It was late enough to go after the mail, and I was beginning to worry a little about Roberta. Anything serious I'd have been informed of, I was sure, but still, it was unlike her not to write faithfully and not to return my call. I hated to go to the post office as grubby as I was, but I really didn't want to change when I wasn't through out here. It wouldn't be the first time I'd showed up there with mud on my knees.

I walked down, as usual, and scooted through the chatterers in the lobby. For once I wasn't interested in the latest gossip. I opened my box, and was relieved to see, among the junk, a familiar blue envelope with the printed return address. I waited until I was again outside and headed up the street to open it. For some reason, from the minute I held it in my hand I was apprehensive.

"Dear Mom," I read in Roberta's precise handwriting. "I should have phoned you, but I thought I'd break the news to you first by letter. Besides, you'll be seeing me soon. I plan to fly out on Friday, if that's all right. Let me know if it isn't."

Get to the point, I thought, my eyes scanning ahead.

I didn't like the point when I got to it. "Joel and I are getting a divorce. This has been a long time coming, but I didn't want to burden you with our problems because I hoped we could work things out. It's an amiable divorce, don't worry that we're screaming and threatening each other. Neither of us is that sort. I'll explain when I see you.

"Don't worry about meeting me at the airport. I want to rent a car anyway, so expect me in the late afternoon Friday, unless I hear from you otherwise. All my love, Roberta."

My hand sagged and so did my heart and I'm afraid my head did, too. What a day this was turning out to be. Police visits and divorces. I've always thought rational people should, as Roberta had put it, be able to "work things out." Divorces are much too easy to obtain, in my opinion. If the two of them weren't angry at each other, why couldn't they make it work? They had so much in common and had been so much in love. At least, Roberta had been. I hadn't known Joel well enough to be sure, but he'd had all the outward appearances of a man deeply in love.

Poor Roberta. My heart lifted just a little, though. Did this mean she was returning to the Seattle area to live? She could easily find work, as talented as she was. Perhaps her former employer would take her back. How nice it would be to have her nearby. We have no other relatives except distant cousins in Arkansas.

I walked in the front door, dropped the other mail on the kitchen table to peruse at lunch and sank into a chair to re-read Roberta's letter. Why couldn't she have said more? Would it do any good to phone? Evidently not, since she hadn't returned my call last night. Well, I'd just have to wait until Friday to hear the details.

It was lunchtime, but I didn't have any appetite. I might as well go outside and finish my work. I wandered over to the milk container where I'd been collecting slugs before Jake had interrupted me. Slugs are surprisingly fast. A number had managed to ooze their way to the top and over the side to freedom. With a little searching, I found most of them.

I carried the carton over to the fence and pushed the usual loose board. I slid the whole thing through, and flipped my hand, in order to dump the slugs.

Suddenly, a crushing weight pressed my wrist to the ground. I cried out, more with surprise than pain, although a large foot pressing one's hand into the dirt doesn't feel good.

I knew instantly what had happened. I'd been careless. I hadn't checked the knothole. I hadn't even glanced at Cyrus's house to see if the curtains were pulled in the telltale manner that indicated he wasn't at home.

"Gotcha!" he said.

97

CHAPTER X

"Surely you realized I'd notice the surplus of slugs near the loose board, didn't you?" Cyrus's voice from the other side of the Berlin Wall sounded fierce, but with an overtone of laughter.

I couldn't blame him, I guess. I had been both foolish and negligent. "You can take your clodhopper off my arm now. How long have you known?"

"Long enough," he said, removing his foot. "And it's not a clodhopper. Actually, it's a very expensive shoe. I find it worthwhile to buy the best in footgear."

"If you knew," I asked, pulling my arm and the container back through the fence and straightening up, "why didn't you just nail the board?"

"Isn't carrying on this conversation through a six-foot fence unnecessarily cumbersome? Why don't you come into my lair for a change? You might even find it interesting."

"I don't think I care to," I said. "I asked you, why didn't you nail the board shut?"

"Because this little charade was much more entertaining, my dear Donna. I knew that sooner or later I'd catch you in the act."

"But, why?" I wailed.

"The days are boring in retirement, don't you find? Anything to liven things up. Life has been much more fun since I moved next door to you."

I stared at the uneven, graying boards between us. I wished I could see his face. Expressions can be so revealing. Although, if I could believe him, I would be the loser in that category.

"I don't even need to ask why you chose to be so generous with your slugs," he said. "I know how angry you were about the fence. Believe me, I didn't plan it to upset you."

"Was that meant to be an apology?"

"No, I don't think so. I don't feel *I* have anything to apologize for. You, however . . ."

"That'll be a cold day in hell," I muttered.

"Donna! I'm shocked. Don't you think we should get together and discuss this?"

"Absolutely not. I wish I didn't have to see your—your puss again."

"Actually, I find the whole situation laughable. Don't you? I won't hold it against you."

Defeated, I slunk away. As I departed, I heard him chuckle and say what I think was, "Humorless woman."

Why, oh, why had fate put me in one house and Cyrus, with his rows of vegetables like soldiers and his high fence and his distorted sense of humor, in the house next door? Yes, he did have a sense of humor, I finally had to admit. It was just that it was—it was peculiar. Who else would laugh at my dismay when my neighbors and friends thought of me in terms of a murderess? Who else would think it was humorous to poke fun at me by naming that darling, sweet cat after me because it was loud? Who else would set me up for humiliation when he knew about the slugs all this time? All he'd had to do was admit he knew I was putting them in his yard. I'd expected him to be angry. That was the purpose of starting the whole thing to begin with. To annoy that supercilious man next door in retaliation.

Maybe I should put my house up for sale, and remove myself forever from Cyrus Bates's territory. But, no. I couldn't let him drive me away. I was here first. Cedar Harbor is my home. If Cyrus had been angry at me, thrown a temper tantrum as I might have expected, the result would have been that we'd ignore each other in the future and go our own ways. Well, so be it. That's what I'd do now. Ignore him totally. And I'd have what I'd wanted in the first place.

Except, said the little voice from inside that's always telling me things whether I want to hear them or not, *he got the best of you.*

The next mistake I made was not being home when Roberta arrived. I had a morning appointment in Seattle with my dentist. If I ever reach the point I can't drive, I'll probably have to give up Dr. Burtt, but I've gone to him for years and he's good, and I don't want to search for another reliable person. Locating a good dentist is so difficult. One doesn't discover if the work is inferior until years later, I've found to my dismay in the past. Dr. Burtt's office is clear downtown in the Cobb Building and getting to it is a nuisance, but there it is. I assumed I'd be back long before Roberta arrived. Late afternoon, she'd said.

As I steered my old green Chevy onto Beach Street, I could see an unfamiliar vehicle parked in front of my house. I wondered about it slightly, but the Moores have tons of company who often park there, so I didn't think much of it. It was, after all, only one-thirty in the afternoon, and the thought that Roberta might have arrived didn't even cross my mind. I pulled into my driveway, opened the garage door with my opener and moved the car inside.

It was only as I twisted the knob on the door going into my kitchen that I heard a voice. That gave me a turn, believe me.

I froze. Almost instantaneously, though, I realized it was Roberta I was hearing. She must be speaking to someone on the phone. I threw open the door and rushed inside.

"Roberta," I said, "you're here. I'm so glad . . ." And then I froze again. Seated at the kitchen table, drinking what was undoubtedly *my* coffee out of *my* mug with cats on it that Roberta had given me, was Cyrus. Playing at his feet was Donna Two.

I'd been so startled to see him that I hardly noticed my beautiful daughter sitting next to him, which says something about how upset I was. "Mom," Roberta said, rising to her feet and coming over and hugging me, "it's good to be here."

"It's good to have you," I said, burying my nose in her dark hair. She smelled good, so familiar. My little girl. I stepped back and searched her face for signs of unhappiness. I didn't see any, except for a few unusual lines that might indicate either fatigue or stress.

"You're looking great, Mom. Trim and tan and healthy. Sorry to get here early. There was a cancellation and I just wanted to get out of New York as soon as I could."

I felt a surge of hope. Did that mean that she truly was ready to return to the Puget Sound area? "I'm sorry I wasn't here," I said. "The empty house . . ."

"Oh," she said, "no problem. Cyrus has been keeping me company and bringing me up to date on what's going on in Cedar Harbor. Why didn't you tell me you had such a charming neighbor?"

"Charming?" My tone made Roberta raise her eyebrows questioningly, and glance at Cyrus. She no doubt considered me rude. Fine. I, too, turned my gaze toward my enemy.

Yes, I suppose superficially one would assume Cyrus was charming. As usual, his dress was immaculate. He had on gray slacks, a muted blue and gray polo shirt and gray walking shoes. Not a spot on anything. His hair, also as usual, was under control, without a strand in disarray. Sometime I'd like to muss it up. Maybe spill something down his front while I was at it. Maybe I could turn the hose on him the next time he complained because I was watering.

"Excellent coffee," he said, waving the kitty-covered mug. "You must have bought the cup in honor of Donna Two."

"Roberta gave it to me. That's my favorite mug." I noticed for the first time that indeed, one of the cats on the mug could have been modeled after the kitten.

"I'll get you a cup of tea." Roberta sprang toward the stove.

"Thank you," I said. "There're some cookies in the old cookie jar." I knew I shouldn't settle down with tea until I got rid of Cyrus, but I needed something. I hadn't had lunch yet, and I felt drained. Not vital like I should. I plunked down at the table, across from Cyrus, but turned back and studied Roberta.

She was thinner, I could see, inspecting her firm behind in the slim blue skirt. Her silk blouse, in a lighter blue, was expensive looking, and the gold that flashed at her ears as she tossed her head was probably real. Her hair was longer than the last time I'd seen her, when she'd had one of those ridiculous cropped styles some young women affect. It was parted now on one side and combed back over her ears into a short pageboy. "I like your hair," I said.

She smiled ruefully over her shoulder. "Joel didn't like the old style."

Joel. Roberta was hiding her feelings, but she must be going through hell. We all want life to turn out well for our children and we have so little control. In my own case, though, fate had determined that Bob and I would not be able to spend life together. I wondered what had happened to

Roberta and Joel's marriage. She'd tell me when she got a chance, when we were alone.

I glanced away, and Cyrus's complacent face intruded on my thoughts and reminded me why, exactly, Roberta was unable to confide at the moment. "Why are you here?" I asked.

Roberta, with a puzzled frown, brought the steaming cup to the table. "Mr. Bates came looking for his cat," she said. "I'd found her playing with a package that was on your front porch. I brought her inside. I had no idea where she belonged."

"She doesn't belong here," I said.

"Well, I thought I should bring her in at least," Roberta said. "Mom, you seem out of sorts. Where have you been?"

"The dentist," I muttered, taking a drink. It was much too hot, and it was all I could muster not to spit it back into the cup.

"No wonder." Her face cleared. "As I was saying, Mr. Bates . . ."

"I asked you to call me Cyrus." He fingered his moustache. Did he intend to look lecherous? If so, he was failing. I started to get up.

"What is it, Mom? I'll get . . . Oh, the cookies," she said. "Let me. You look tired."

Great. A few minutes ago she was complimenting me on how good I looked. That's what sitting across the table from Cyrus could do. I settled back down and let her wait on me, wondering why Cyrus, whose manners were usually of the best, didn't have the courtesy to leave.

He must have picked up my vibes. "I'll be going," he said, pushing the cup to one side.

"Oh, please finish your coffee," Roberta said, her dimple showing. "Mom and I'll have lots of time to talk later. You have to have one of Mom's cookies." I frowned, but she turned away. She rummaged in the jar shaped like a mouse that we've had since she was a tiny girl, and pulled out some of my oatmeal cookies. Not the most beautiful ones in the world, but good for you. I hadn't baked them for Cyrus. She put them on a plate and brought them to the table, on the way picking up a package from the counter.

"Here," she said. "This was lying on the mat at the front door. The torn paper is courtesy of Donna Two."

At mention of her name, the kitten bellowed. Roberta laughed. "She really is darling."

"Darling," I echoed dryly. "I wonder what this is?" I turned the package over, looking for writing, but it hadn't been addressed in any way. It wasn't hard to unwrap, what with the damage already inflicted by the cat. I slid the string off the brown paper and completed the removal of the covering. Inside was a box that had held chocolates, but clearly had seen better days and was undoubtedly being recycled. I lifted the lid.

"Oh," I said, pleased. "Those wonderful lemon crisp cookies. Carrie must have found out who made them for the Historical Society and told her how much I like them. Just in time. Here." I lifted two of the luscious, enticing sweets out of the box and reached to set them on top of the plain oatmeal ones.

"Don't." Cyrus's voice was sharp as he stretched his hand to intercept mine. "I don't think that's a good idea."

"What?" Roberta asked, looking startled.

A creepy, crawly sensation traveled down my spine. I knew what Cyrus was going to say before he said it. "When one person has been poisoned already from gift food, don't you think it would be a good idea to be sure where these came from before you eat them?" His fingers on my hand were firm.

"Mom?" Roberta's expression was horrified.

CHAPTER XI

I ignored the shaky feeling that lingered in my spine and retrieved my hand. "Aren't you overreacting, Cyrus?" I asked.

"Overreacting? Hardly. Marie Corrigan was in the hospital several days. Another time the poisoner would be more likely to make sure. Figuring the dosage of how much monkshood would kill a person must be difficult for an amateur, which I'm assuming our villain is. A little experimenting might be in order. There must be a point, also, where the food would become unpalatable, and the poisoner can't, after all, taste it to find out."

"But why would anyone want to poison my mother?" Roberta asked, her voice shaky.

"That's a good question, Cyrus. Why would anyone be interested in killing me? I've never done anything reprehensible enough to cause that much anger, I assure you. And my connections with the Corrigan family are so tenuous . . . I was on the water board with Lyle, taught Jolene and Lyle, Junior, and see Marie once in a while in public. What about that could possibly cause anyone to poison me?"

"Why would anyone deliver the cookies anonymously?"

"They weren't . . ." I scrabbled through the wrappings, hoping to find something to indicate the package's source so I could prove him wrong. Nothing but the proverbial plain, brown wrapper. "Oh, for heaven's sake. Maybe whoever it was just wanted to surprise me with something nice. I can't go through life being paranoid about everything. Maybe that's the kind of life you saw in your years in the Navy, but *I* have spent my adulthood in Cedar Harbor, and things don't work that way here."

"They don't? What about Lyle, and Marie, and Jolene?"

"This is ridiculous," Roberta pleaded. "Will someone please explain?"

Cyrus glanced at me, eyebrows lifted. "Isn't it about time you tell your daughter everything that's going on in Cedar Harbor?"

"I thought you'd already taken care of that for me," I snapped.

"Hardly. I didn't think it was my place to inform her that you imagined you were the center of attention the other day in regard to the poison."

"Imagine? Imagine?" My voice was becoming shrill, and I swallowed, trying to regain my composure.

"Mom, you wrote that Mrs. Corrigan had been poisoned, but what does that have to do with you?" Roberta's face was pale and lined with worry. Darn Cyrus for doing this, I thought.

"That is a very good question." Cyrus focused purposefully on Roberta. "Somehow your mother has been involved in this whole thing since she was intemperate enough to find Lyle Corrigan's body on the beach at dawn."

I slammed my mug down, sloshing tea on the table. "Cyrus Bates, that is truly one of the most illogical, irresponsible statements . . ."

"Mother!" Roberta interrupted. "*Please* tell me what's going on."

I exhaled, feeling my body slump in response. "I don't know," I said. "I wish I did. I feel involved—I'm not sure why. I feel as if I'm being swept along by events that are out of my control."

"Don't be dramatic, Donna," Cyrus said. "You involved yourself. You did that when you went to Marie about Jolene's return instead of going to the police."

"I've heard everything about that episode that I want to hear. Why don't you go home? And take your—your pet with you." We all turned to look at Donna Two, who was attempting to shred the bamboo blind that hung over half of my sliding door.

Roberta shot me a look of reproach, bounced from her chair and retrieved the kitten as Cyrus, too, stood. "I'm going," he said, "but I truly recommend that you let me take a sample of cookies to be analyzed before you eat them. Better safe than sorry."

"Why not the police? How can you . . ."

"I told you earlier, I have contacts from my Navy days. I didn't spend my time running around on a PT boat, you know. And as to why not the police, can you picture Chief Donniker if you approached him with a batch of lemon crisp cookies someone had given you and asked him to have them analyzed?"

Now I really wilted. "Yes, I can picture him quite well. I still think you're wrong, but . . . I suppose I should thank you," I said as Roberta handed him first Donna Two and then the three cookies, which she wrapped in a paper napkin and put in a baggie.

I couldn't tell whether his answering grin was sardonic or larded with humor or both. "You can thank me if it turns out I'm right."

"Shouldn't we stick the rest in the freezer just in case?" Roberta asked. "We can eat them later if they're okay."

"I don't think I'd enjoy them," I said. "I'd wonder what

might be in a cookie that was missed. Unless, of course, I can find out where they came from, who made them. It may be a simple gesture of goodwill."

"Maybe," Cyrus said, sounding as if he didn't really agree. "But if so, why wasn't there a card enclosed to tell you where they came from?"

"I don't know."

He left then, carrying the cookies and the cat. Roberta slipped an arm around my shoulder from behind and hugged me. "Mom," she asked, "have you had lunch?"

"No, as a matter of fact. Why?"

"You always get grumpy when you don't eat, you know."

"Oh, come on. Food isn't important to me."

"Maybe not, but let me fix something?"

"I have a better idea. Why don't we go down to the Inn for lunch in honor of your being here? It's late and it won't be crowded, and I'll tell you all about the Corrigans and Cyrus. And the miserable water board. And you can tell me about the divorce."

"Not something I enjoy talking about." Her mouth twisted. "But I must, I suppose, and I do love eating at the Inn. Let's go."

I was right about the restaurant not being crowded. Alissa was on duty again, and she led us to a nice corner table overlooking the harbor. "Perfect," I said. "Alissa, have you met my daughter, Roberta Schwartz?"

"No, I haven't." Alissa handed us our menus. "How do you do, Mrs. Schwartz. Are you here for a while?"

How like Alissa to ask.

Roberta smiled. "No, just a short visit. Were you one of my mother's pupils?"

"Yeah." Alissa didn't elaborate. Oh, well, I was, no doubt,

not Alissa's favorite teacher, and although I'd liked the girl—
one couldn't help enjoying her ebullient personality—my favorite pupils tended to be ones who were more interested in
being in school than she had been. Yes, I admit to having fa-
vorites. All teachers would if they were honest. Even back
then, nine or ten years ago, it was obvious that being a waitress might be Alissa's highest career goal, until she married,
of course, and achieved the nirvana that girls of that age la-
mentably still think a man will provide.

She bustled off to bring us each a glass of Chardonnay,
and we ordered before we settled down with the wine for a
much-needed discussion.

"You, first, Mom." Roberta gestured with her glass.
"What's going on in your life is obviously more interesting
than my boring old divorce."

"I wouldn't say that. I'm . . ."

"Begin with why you're feuding with that handsome man
next door," she interrupted. "You told me about the fence
when he put it in, but that hardly seems enough to make you
quite so angry."

She obviously wasn't ready to begin her own story. Well,
I'd give her time. "Handsome is as handsome does," I said. "I
thought I taught you that as a small child."

"You did." Her dimple was evident. "But there were a few
other lessons about forgiveness."

"Humph." I paused, wondering how on earth I was going
to explain to my daughter about the slugs. In retrospect, the
whole thing seemed childish and foolish.

Nevertheless, I dove in and gave her the entire story of
Cyrus. As she has always done, she listened without inter-
rupting until I got to the activities of yesterday. When I explained how Cyrus had trapped my arm with his foot, she
choked on her wine.

An alarmed Alissa arrived and handed her a napkin as Roberta struggled to stop coughing. "Are you all right, Mrs. Schwartz?" she asked, looking appalled.

Roberta nodded, and squeaked, "Just fine. Thank you, Alissa." She took the napkin and buried her face for a moment. Then one brown eye peaked out. "Is she gone?" she whispered.

"Yes." Alissa had been summoned by someone who had gestured from the door of the kitchen.

She dropped the napkin on the table. "Oh, Mom," she said, reaching in her purse for a tissue and wiping her eyes, "that is absolutely the funniest thing I have ever heard."

"Funny? Childish, maybe, but I don't see anything funny in the situation at all."

"Later," she said. "It'll be funny later."

I thought it wise not to tell her that Cyrus had accused me of having no sense of humor. "Let's forget that man," I said. "I really want to excise him from my life."

"And how are you going to do that?" she asked. "I mean, aside from living next door to him, having his cat wander into your yard, being on the—didn't you say you were on the water board with him?" I nodded. "Well, aside from that, are you going to tell him to go away when he shows up with the analysis of the cookies?"

I sighed. "I don't suppose I can."

"Well, then. Tell me the rest of the news."

Alissa showed up with our entrees just then. She slid the plate of butter clams in front of Roberta, set my alder-smoked salmon at my place, then left. The food appeared especially appetizing today. Maybe because of the company.

"Look at the cormorant." She pointed at the long-necked black bird perched on a piling next to a particularly scrumptious yacht. "And look there. I do believe that's the same seagull sitting on the same post as the last time I was here."

I smiled, noticing how her face had lost some of the look of strain that I'd seen earlier. Coming here had been a good idea. Or maybe my story inadvertently giving her something to laugh about had done it. Whatever. "The Chamber of Commerce has a contract," I said. "Garbage in exchange for looking picturesque."

"Oh, it's so good to be here." She forked a clam, dipped it in the melted butter and popped it into her mouth. "Well, go on, tell me what else has happened."

I proceeded to, and as before, she listened attentively. When I got to the part about Jolene, she said, "I remember her. She was just a couple of years behind me. I don't remember her very well, but she was a friend of that girl who committed suicide. Mary Larson. I've never forgotten that. Death makes a big impression when you're fourteen."

"Yes, I know. The school year was never the same. The whole school was affected, not just my class. But my kids were upset the most, of course. Nowadays they bring in counselors, but then I just did the best I could, and I knew it wasn't enough."

She placed a hand on mine. "I know you, Mom. I'll bet you did just what was right. Understanding tempered with, 'Let's get on with what needs doing.' "

I nodded. I'd never thought of my methods, but that would come pretty close to describing them.

"And no one knows where Jolene is?" Roberta asked. "How sad."

"No, they don't. And, while Chief Donniker could be right that she murdered her father and then took off for unknown places, I seriously doubt it. I truly fear the worst. But now . . ." I hesitated, hating to introduce a subject that would again make her unhappy.

She must have known what I was thinking, as she so often does, because she began, "It's my turn, isn't it? You'd like to know what's up with Joel and me." She smiled ruefully, "Or maybe I should say, 'what's down.' As I told you, problems have been developing for a long time."

"But you had so much in common. The plays, the concerts, reading . . ."

"It may have looked that way. Our biggest problem, though, was that he's a dedicated workaholic. My job's important to me, too, but so was my marriage, and it just wasn't to him. I didn't tell you how many of those plays and concerts I saw with friends while Joel went back to the office. And reading? Who needs company to read? Most nights I sat alone with a book. But let's not talk about him. I came home—and I want to put him out of my mind for these three weeks."

"Only three weeks? I'd hoped that you'd come back to stay. You love it here so."

"I do. And I'd love to be closer to you, too. But I adore my job and I've worked my way up. I'd have to start all over here and I don't want to do that. Besides, there aren't too many jobs in publishing in the Northwest."

"New York may not be as appealing, living on one salary."

"It'll be hard. But we'll sell the condo and I'll find a small apartment. I have friends there. Don't worry about me, Mom. I've always taken care of myself and I will now."

She took a sip of water, then patted my hand. "Now back to you. What did Cyrus mean about you being the center of attention concerning the poisoning? Or not being, as the case may be?"

Reluctantly I explained. "And they *were* staring at me, no matter what he says."

And, just as I had expected, she tried to convince me that it was only because of my knowledge of plant life. Almost word for word as I had envisioned the conversation. Then she added, "Cyrus seems to be such a sensible man. I really do think you should listen to him."

With great effort, I restrained the retort that came naturally to my lips. "You'll find out," I muttered, "if you're here long enough."

"Do you know anything about plant poisons?" she asked curiously.

"Now I do. I took out a couple of books from the library. Strange how one can go in there and check out a recipe for murder. It was fascinating reading, though. Most everything I grow could be poisonous. There are even histories of the famous cases. Anyone could read up and acquire the information needed."

"Nowadays they'd look it up on the Internet, Mom. I've been trying to persuade you to get with it."

I made a face. "So I can look up poisons?" I waved Alissa away with her tray of tempting desserts. They were much too rich after a lunch larger than either of us would normally eat. "Cyrus does wear one down, but now that I've had time to think about it, the more convinced I am that he was wrong," I said. "And I know how to prove it. When I get home, I'm going to get on the phone and track down those cookies. That's all I need, to find out who sent them.

"And it will," I added with a touch of maliciousness, "give me great pleasure to tell Cyrus that he's wrong. I doubt if that happened to him much in his days in the Navy."

"I hope you're right," Roberta said, holding up her coffee cup to indicate to Alissa that she wanted a refill.

CHAPTER XII

We wandered down onto the town dock after we finished eating. Today the tide was in and the water almost serene, lapping gently on the beach with the relaxing sound of pebbles being tumbled and slowly water-worn. We'd each saved our roll from the Inn and we amused ourselves for a few minutes tossing bits to voracious seagulls.

"Where was . . . Lyle Corrigan when you found him, Mom?" Roberta knew where I usually go clam digging.

"Right out there." I pointed to the left. "Not very far. His body evidently was put in here from the dock. You know how the current always drifts a boat in that direction on an outgoing tide."

She nodded. "Stronger than anybody'd think. I remember being caught there that time in a canoe. I was scared. And humiliated when I had to be rescued."

"I've wondered whether his body was brought to the dock and thrown in or whether he was shot right here. He could have even been in a boat with his murderer, I suppose. I haven't heard what the police think." I didn't comment on why the police and I hardly communicated these days.

"I never liked him much," she said. "The way he looked at me sometimes—he just gave me the creeps. But I guess he was okay. Everybody else seemed to think so. Anyway, that's not the point. It's not right in my book to shoot someone, no matter what."

"Nor mine," I said. "Well. Shall we head on home? You must be tired."

"Not really. But I need to unpack. You've had a long day, too." She suddenly hugged me. "Thanks, Mom."

"That's nice, but for what?"

"For being here."

We grinned foolishly at each other, then turned and strolled toward home.

Roberta looked at everything we passed. "I do love Cedar Harbor," she said. "At night sometimes, when the sirens are blaring and I can hear street noises, I think about it. There's so much building going on here, though. It's changing. That was an empty lot the last time I was here, and so was that one." She pointed to two pristine new dwellings, one still for sale.

"Well, construction has slowed down now, because we aren't sure about the water supply. I never dreamed when I accepted a position on the water board what would be involved." I told her about Mark Gasper and Shadybrook Meadows. And about Al Parry.

"Hmm," she commented. "Paying a bribe doesn't seem very wise to me. I mean, aside from the legalities. It could backfire. At least, if I were on the board, I'd be inclined to vote against the man if I thought he'd been influencing people that way."

"I agree. And so does Michael Jarvis, I think, and, I hate to admit, Cyrus. The only thing is, we have absolutely no evidence that money changed hands, and the development has some merit. If one accepts that we should let more building here at all. I'm not sure we have the right to keep people out, though, just because we like Cedar Harbor the way it is. As you can see, I, at least, have mixed feelings."

We approached Cyrus's house and that reminded me.

"Cyrus said he was going to investigate why the county changed its mind about the water moratorium. I'd forgotten. Anyway, I assumed that he was just talking through his hat. But now I'm not so sure. Maybe he did do something more useful in the Navy than seeing the world on some warship."

"Mom, I think you don't know much about the military these days. Oh. There he is." She waved gaily toward his house where, out of the corner of my eye, I could see him standing in the front window watching us. I pretended I didn't see him.

"The military is a whole community," she went on. "One could have a career in almost any field and still be a member of the armed forces. He could be a lawyer, or an investigator . . ."

"Or a cook, or a member of a band. I know, Roberta. I'm not quite that behind on things. I just prefer to ignore the military establishment." I stooped to pull a weed which had sprouted in the bed of roses lining the front of my place.

"You know me better than that." Roberta waited patiently as I removed yet another. "Knowledge is power. I've never had much patience with people who don't vote and don't pay attention to what congress is doing . . ."

"Or not doing."

". . . or not doing. Yes. That's equally important."

I pressed a hand to my back as I straightened. "I'm getting too old for this."

She laughed. "You'll never be too old to garden."

We started up my front walk and I returned to our conversation. "I'm glad to see I brought you up right. As if I'd had any doubts. Just so you know, though, I have never missed an election since my twenty-first birthday. No, that's not right. My gall bladder chose an inopportune time to go on a rampage and I missed one. I actually thought, lying in my hos-

116

pital bed, of trying to get an absentee ballot, but somehow pushing the button to give myself enough pain killer seemed more important at the time."

"I'm sorry, Mom. I didn't mean to sound patronizing."

"I know that."

As I unlocked the front door, the phone began to ring. I dropped my purse in a chair, and hurried to get it. I had to argue with my answering machine to get through, but that out of the way, I heard Al Parry's imperious tones.

"Thought you weren't going to answer," the unmistakable voice began accusingly.

Not for the first time, I wondered why I had allowed my sense of civic duty to lead me into having to deal with Al. "I just came in the door," I said courteously, as always trying to set an example.

"Hmmph. Well. You know we need two good people to go on the board next month."

"Yes. Of course." I wondered if his idea of a good person and mine would ever be the same.

"Found one," he said. "At least I think so. You'll be glad to have another woman."

"Indeed," I answered noncommittally.

"I was talking to that young woman. Friend of yours, I understand. Susan Reilly?"

"What? Oh, you must be mistaken. I've asked her myself and she absolutely refused."

"No, I'm not mistaken. She said she'd been thinking about it and decided she should do her share."

"Well, I'll be darned." I tuned Al out as I thought. Yes, Sue would be a good member and would surely tip the scales toward sanity. But what had made her change her mind?

"... and we'll need one more," he finished what he'd been saying. "Got any ideas?"

"Uh . . . no, not really." If I could be so wrong about one candidate, I doubted my judgment in picking another. Still . . . "A thought did just occur to me. Would it be too soon, I mean . . . ?" I knew I was being unusually incoherent.

"Donna, I'm not a mind-reader."

"Oh, I realize that. It's just that . . . Well, I was wondering about Lyle, Junior. I mean, Will Corrigan. Is he here in town to stay, do you know? He seems sensible." Actually, I didn't know any such thing from our one brief encounter in the hardware store. I was operating from gut feeling. He'd been very different from his father as a youngster. Surely as an adult, he wouldn't be another Lyle?

"He's here to stay. He's taking over the store. Not a bad idea." Al sounded so approving that I immediately became suspicious. Had I created an unnecessary problem?

"I'll get on it right away," he said. "And, uh, thanks." Oh, how that man hated to admit I could come up with any good suggestion at all. If it was.

"You're welcome," I said dourly as I heard the click that indicated he'd already hung up. No ceremony for Al. He'd said neither hello nor goodbye.

"I've got to phone Sue," I said, turning around.

"Fine, Mom," Roberta said. "I'll go unpack while you're on the phone. Mind if I set up the ironing board?"

"Of course not. This is your home."

She smiled and disappeared down the hall toward her old room, which remained the way it was when she left for college, a mix of pink ruffled spread, athletic trophies from her swim team and posters of rock stars. I had left it for her to keep or change when she was ready.

I punched in the digits to call Sue. Fortunately, I remember numbers easily. I feel so for those who must constantly look in the phone book to make a call, especially if they're old enough to need to find their glasses first as I do. The phone rang three times before Sue answered. "Hello?" Her voice was welcoming.

"Sue," I said as I settled in a chair. "This is Donna. What's this about you volunteering for the water board?"

"I didn't volunteer. Al Parry saw me at Thrifty and asked me."

"Are you nuts?"

"Only as nuts as you are. You're on the thing."

"Yes, I'm aware I am, believe me. But I didn't really know what I was getting into and, thanks to me, you do. Besides, you told me you wouldn't do it and you said you couldn't afford the babysitter."

"I did." Her voice bubbled with laughter. "Can't a person change her mind?"

"Of course. And you know I'll be very glad to have you there beside me. But I hate to have it cost you, when you'd rather use your babysitting for joining your string quartet."

"Oh, I won't be giving my group up," she said. "It's taken care of."

Her tone of voice was distinctly evasive. Taken care of? I didn't like the sound of that. By whom? I couldn't exactly ask, any more than I'd already probed. "Well, it's good of you. And we all do have to take on distasteful tasks at times."

"Exactly my feelings. You're such a good example, Donna. I just decided it was my turn."

"Well, thanks. By the way, my daughter's home for a visit. Drop by some afternoon. I don't think you've met."

"I'd enjoy that."

I hung up the phone slowly. Something wasn't right. Sue really was on a tight budget. She'd practically spelled out the figures on previous occasions. What had made her change her mind? I hated to be suspicious of everyone's motives, but how could one help it these days?

I shrugged and turned away from the phone. It was only as I stood and headed down the hall to see how Roberta was coming along that I suddenly remembered something that gave me a chill. I had a clear view of Sue, her head down next to Mark Gasper's as she sat and chatted with him at the Historical Society meeting. She'd praised the man before, saying how helpful he'd been since her husband died.

Was Mark being helpful again? At the very least, was he paying for her babysitter? Or, worse yet, had her acceptance of a position on the water board been his idea from the beginning?

I stopped in the hall and ran a hand through my hair as I thought. How could I find out?

CHAPTER XIII

The conversations with Al and Susan completely sidetracked my intent to track down the cookies. It was only after Roberta and I had a light meal of soup and crackers and I reached for the mouse jar that I remembered.

"Oh," I said. "I was going to call around about those lemon crisp cookies. I'll do it this evening. That is, do you have something to do for a few minutes? I wouldn't be neglecting you?"

"Of course not. Actually, that mystery I started on the airplane is good and I wouldn't mind finishing it. You go ahead. I'll load the dishwasher."

I phoned Carrie first, since I had spoken to her about the recipe. We chatted for a moment, and then I asked, "Did you by chance find out who brought those cookies I liked so much to the Historical Society meeting?"

"As a matter of fact, I did. It was Bessie Amherst. I didn't have a chance to ask her about the recipe, though. Noreen Parry was in charge of refreshments that day and I only checked with her to see if she remembered who'd brought them."

"Terrific," I said, as my mind puzzled over the information. "Thanks loads, Carrie. I'll call and ask her for the recipe."

"You're welcome. Glad I was able to help."

Carrie was feeling talkative, as she often does, not being as

121

used to living alone as I am. We rehashed Jolene's continued absence and she wanted to know all about Mark Gasper's development. It was difficult to get away from her without being abrupt. But finally, to my relief, she said, "Oh. Someone's at the door. I'll be seeing you."

I said goodbye and hung up. Bessie Amherst? That elderly founder of the group whom I knew only from the meetings? She couldn't possibly be the one who sent me the package, but I'd call to see what I could find out anyway. I had to find my glasses to look her number up in the club directory, but then soon was answered by a quavery male voice. "Hello?"

I asked for Bessie and the voice, no doubt belonging to her husband, asked, "Who's calling?"

"Donna Galbreath."

"Who?"

Oh, for heaven's sake. "From the Historical Society," I said.

I must have been making faces, because Roberta looked up from her book, laughing. I grimaced.

Once Bessie got to the phone, I was able to get to the point quickly. "Oh, those wonderful cookies," she said in answer to my query. "I got the recipe from Gloria Larson."

Ahah. Odd how often her name turned up these days. Her I could see as a poisoner. But I couldn't see her as sending me a gift, and that was surely what the cookies would turn out to be. "Someone left me a box of the lemon crisps," I said, "and I don't know who."

"Well, it wasn't me. You must have a secret friend." She cackled. It's odd, what happens to voices when one reaches true old age. "I'll get the recipe for you now, though, if you'd like."

"Oh, that's all right, Bessie," I said. "If you'd just bring a copy to the next meeting you come to, I'd appreciate it. I was thinking ahead to Christmas baking."

"All right. Next month. Oh, no. I have to miss that meeting. Stewart's having a hip replacement."

What does one say to that? Is it good news or bad news? Finally, I settled for, "Well, best of luck to him."

"September," she said. "I'll bring it without fail in September. In fact, I'll go copy it right now so I don't forget."

"That would be lovely, Bessie," I said, wishing we could end the conversation.

"It's so easy to forget when you get to be eighty-six years old," she said.

"Oh, you're teasing. You can't possibly be that old."

"Yes, indeed. Eighty-six."

Finally I managed to put an end to our chat. By now, Roberta had laid down her book and was openly laughing. "You're more entertaining than reading. I take it it's not easy? But you found out who made the cookies?"

"No." I sighed in frustration. "One more person to call." I dialed Gloria, wondering, though, how I could possibly phrase tactfully asking whether she had sent a gift or perhaps had tried to poison me.

This conversation stayed mercifully on the subject. "Lemon crisp?" she asked in answer to my inquiry as to whether she had given the recipe to Bessie. I pretended, of course, that I hadn't spoken directly with the old lady. "Sure. I remember. I gave it to her. That's because she lost her cookbook the Historical Society put out, was it ten years ago? She asked in the meeting if anyone still had one because she wanted to make those cookies. I don't think I ever baked them myself, though."

Oh, great. At least I didn't have to ask her if she'd sent the gift. "Guess I missed that meeting," I said.

"I could hunt the recipe up for you," she offered, her tone begrudging, "but you've probably got that book yourself. Don't you remember? We all contributed."

"Um, yes. I'm sure I do. I just didn't think to look in it. Thanks, Gloria," I said.

"Did you find out anything useful?" Roberta asked as I hung up the phone.

"Only that anyone and everyone had access to the recipe—it's in a book we all have, even me, which makes it hopeless to track down the package. I mean, *if* the cookies have anything wrong with them, which I doubt. Otherwise, I can ask at the next meeting, and if I find out they were a genuine gift, well, then we can take them out of the freezer and eat them. Did Cyrus say how long this analysis was going to take?"

"Only that he didn't know."

"What a nuisance."

We enjoyed the next few days. Roberta said she wanted to do all the touristy things, so we went to Deception Pass and leaned over the railing of that frightfully high bridge and watched the current rush through as the tide changed. We went shopping at LaConner, and at lunchtime we were able to snare a table behind the bakery on the old dock overlooking the slough. It's so entertaining watching the yachts and fishing boats slowly churn by on their way to and from the San Juan Islands. One day we joined the throngs of tourists at the restored Pioneer Square in Seattle and finished up the afternoon at the Pike Place Market, coming home with freshly-caught salmon and an array of just-harvested vegetables.

That was the evening that Will Corrigan phoned. "Mrs. Galbreath," he inquired. "I mentioned to you that day in the store that I hoped you'd stop by and see my mother."

"Well, yes, but I thought you were just being polite. I mean, I greatly fear that your mother is less than happy with me, and justifiably so."

"Oh, that," he said. "No, she recognizes that she should have gone to the police herself. You were entirely right. But, Mom . . . Mom is really keeping too much to herself. She's worried about Jolene, we both are, and she's grieving for my father, of course."

I noticed that he didn't include himself in the latter.

"I know it's a lot to ask, but Mom really doesn't have any close friends. I'm afraid Dad saw to that. And I have so much respect for you. I just thought . . ."

"Oh course, Will, I'm sorry I didn't do it without being prompted. My daughter Roberta is here . . ."

"Oh, you're too busy."

"No, what I was going to say was that I feel sure that Roberta would be happy to go with me. She remembers Jolene, and you, of course. Let's see. Weren't you just a year or so older than Roberta?"

"Yes. Say hello to her. I remember her well. She had the fattest ponytail in the school and she always said what she thought. I was actually in Spanish class with her."

So I did, and that was how we found ourselves the next morning parking the Chevy on the curving driveway in front of the Corrigan manor. Roberta looked around curiously. "I've never been here," she said. "Fancy, isn't it?"

I agreed as we stepped up on the porch and rang the bell. "At least it must not seem as empty, if Will is living here," I whispered, glad I had when the door opened almost immediately.

A pert young blond, dressed in a black maid's uniform, opened the door. One doesn't see many of those in Cedar Harbor. "Mrs. Corrigan is expecting us," I told her.

"Come in, please. She's in the study."

We followed her down the hall to a door on the left, which stood open. Marie was seated behind a large mahogany desk, but she rose as we entered. "So nice of you to call," she said graciously. "We'll have coffee in here, Morgan. Or tea?"

Roberta chose coffee and I my usual tea, and Morgan departed.

"I thought this would be cozier." Marie waved a hand toward a marble-faced fireplace where a small fire burned. "Please excuse the clutter though," she said, and I glanced at the stacks of papers on the desk and the opened file drawer. Following my glance, she pushed the drawer shut. "There's so much to go through, with Lyle gone. I had so little to do with business . . . but I'll learn," she said bravely.

Something in her manner reminded me of a kid whistling in the dark to keep demons away.

Marie smiled at Roberta. "How nice of you to come with your mother. You live in New York, now, I understand? I did, too, for a couple of years before my marriage. I miss it."

Personally, from my occasional visit there to see Roberta, I have never understood the attraction of that city, the hold it seems to have on people. They chatted about places and activities as Morgan arrived with a tray with our drinks and some cookies. I assessed the plate quickly. No lemon crisps, thank goodness. But what if the cookies here had also been a gift? My gaze met Roberta's. She was thinking the same thing. We'd both pass, I was sure.

I let them carry the conversation as our drinks were distributed, and studied Marie. She looked better than she had the previous time when I had accosted her here at her home, but not a lot. If one only listened to her voice, she sounded perfectly normal, but signs of strain were evident in the tremor in her hand. Her dark eyes were sunken. What else should I have

126

expected? I'd look the same, I'm sure, if Roberta had disappeared under suspicious circumstances. How glad I was that Will had returned to make Marie's life easier.

"Won't you try my cookies?" Marie asked. "I baked them myself this morning."

Ahah. Marie had been astute enough to pick up on our reluctance to eat in her household. "I'd love to." I reached toward the plate.

Roberta, too, accepted a cookie. "Delicious," she said after taking a bite. "You must use real butter."

"Of course." Marie raised an eyebrow.

The conversation lagged then, and I asked quietly, "No word from Jolene?"

"No," she said, "and I've . . . practically reconciled myself to foul play. Jolene wouldn't do this to me."

Wouldn't she? What about all the years she'd stayed away from Cedar Harbor?

"Especially after that vicious attack on me," she went on.

"What a terrible thing that was," I said. "Have you any idea who sent you poisoned food? Lasagna I think I heard?"

"Yes, lasagna." She spit the word out as if it were the distasteful food itself. "I don't think I can ever eat anything Italian again. And, no. I haven't the slightest idea. I never did anything to anybody. That's been my problem sometimes, trying to avoid trouble." She chuckled dryly. "That came out a bit muddled, but you know what I mean."

Sort of. Yes, I was sure that was her character, but of course I really didn't know what trouble specifically she was referring to. Perhaps if I did—if anyone did—the answer to why she had been poisoned would be clear.

"You're looking for answers in Lyle's papers?" I asked, being, I knew, blunt as always.

I saw Roberta look sideways at me in reproach, but Marie

didn't seem to notice. "Of course not," she said, her eyes round and innocent. Too innocent. I glanced toward the fireplace, but the last of a pile of papers in the back that I had noted when we first entered the room was now ashes.

Again she spotted the direction of my glance, and must have realized what I was thinking. "I'm burning some things, yes, but doesn't everyone have papers they mustn't send to recycling these days? So much easier than the shredder, I think. Anyway, I've always preferred my privacy, and so did Lyle. I thought that tackling this myself was the last thing I could do for him. I was married to Lyle for forty-two years, you know."

"Forty-two years," Roberta mused, "and I'm going to make only six."

Marie glanced at her appraisingly. "Oh?"

"Yes, it's no secret. I'm in the midst of a divorce. I know what you mean about papers," she said. "I'll have so much to clear out. Old bank statements and receipts. Why do we keep so much, I wonder?"

Marie chuckled and visibly relaxed. "Please have another cookie," she suggested.

"But, Marie," I persisted, "someone must have thought there was a reason to poison you. What a horrible feeling for you, to know that someone out there must . . . must want to see you dead."

"The doctors aren't sure of that," she said. "The dose made me very ill, but it wasn't life-threatening. Felt like it at the time, of course."

"Could they have been warning you, or . . ."

"Mom," Roberta said, "have another cookie."

What she really wanted me to do was to shut up, and she was, no doubt, right. I'd done enough damage in this household already. I took another chocolate chip.

But, surprisingly, Marie kept on the subject. "I've thought about it," she said, "often. Hate, or warning . . . But, of what? Or maybe, to get even with me. But I'm just not the sort of person who ever steps on toes."

"That's true," I assured her. "I don't think you have a mean bone in your body, and you're always tactful. I'm sorry for even asking. It's just that it's such a puzzle, and I guess puzzles intrigue me."

"I don't mind," Marie said. "I hope someone can come up with an answer, something that might be a clue to what has happened to my daughter. I don't really hold out much hope. That is, the police don't seem to be doing . . ." Always tactful, just as I said. She wasn't about to actually criticize Chief Donniker.

"Well, then," I said, musing, "if you can bear one more question?" She nodded, so I barged right ahead. "Had you started going through Lyle's papers when you were attacked? Or, more to the point, had you mentioned to anyone that you were going to?"

She froze, her hand in mid-air as it reached for a cookie. "I—I had begun," she said. "I remember specifically because I worried while I was in the hospital about leaving the work scattered all over the study. I don't remember though, whether I had told anyone what I was doing. I'll have to think about it. But—Lyle's papers? They're mostly about the hard-ware store."

Why did I have a sudden feeling that she was not being to-tally truthful?

"But maybe someone *thinks* there's something. I'm not even sure, now that you mention it . . . It almost seems that they weren't in the same order . . . But that's easily ex-plained," she said with determination. "After all, Will had come home, and of course the housecleaner had been here. I saw no evidence that anything was missing. I'm glad you suggested that, Donna. Someone did murder my husband, after all, and I have no idea why. I think," she narrowed her eyes as she spoke, "that I'll spread the word that I've finished. That won't be difficult. Then maybe I can get over fearing that someone may try to kill me again, that he or she just misjudged the first time."

Marie was no fool, I reflected. Perhaps everyone had misjudged *her* all these years, and we would see a new Marie when this was all over.

"This must be so distressing for you," Roberta said, rising and grasping Marie's hand. "I do hope you have news of Jolene soon. Mom, hadn't we better be going?"

I brushed off a few crumbs of cookies, set down my half-full tea cup and stood also. Roberta was urging me out the door like a persistent sheepdog.

"If there is anything I can do to help, Marie," I offered, "please let me know."

"You might begin," Marie suggested with a twinkle to her eyes that was definitely new, "by casually mentioning our visit to anyone you happen to be talking to. You might say something to the effect that you caught me as I was just finishing the task of going through Lyle's papers. Something like that, anyway."

"Good idea. I'd be happy to." I was already embellishing the sentence in my mind, about how boring the paperwork was and how relieved Marie was to have it all behind her.

"Still," Roberta interjected, "if you remember mentioning that you were working on your husband's papers to anyone, well, wouldn't it be a good idea to tell the police?"

"I will," Marie promised.

"Tell Jake," I said firmly. "Jake Santorini. Not Chief Donniker."

★ ★ ★ ★ ★

We had barely returned home when the doorbell rang. It was noon, an unlikely hour for anyone to call, and it was too late for UPS. "Get that, will you please?" I called to Roberta from the bathroom, always my first stop after a morning spent drinking tea.

I adjusted my clothing and came out hastily, to find Cyrus standing just inside the door, his expression serious as he spoke. "Hello, Donna."

I knew instantly why he was here, even before my gaze dropped to the envelope he held in one hand. "You got the report," I said unnecessarily, perhaps wanting to stall.

"I got the report." He echoed my words. "There was enough poison in just one cookie to kill all of us. It was the same poison used on Marie."

I sank into the nearest chair. For one of the rare times in my life, I was speechless.

CHAPTER XIV

"Mom," Roberta asked, "are you okay?"

Her question helped me find my voice again. "Yes, of course," I said. "I'm just . . . stunned."

"I'm not sure why," Cyrus said. "It was so obvious."

"Oh, Cyrus," I said. "Spare me. Above all else, don't say, 'I told you so.' Yes, I was wrong and you were right. Okay?"

"Just wanted to hear you say it." He preened that miserable moustache.

"I'm so grateful that you were here," Roberta said. "If you hadn't been, Mom and I would have taken it for granted that some friend had sent the cookies and we'd both be dead."

"Not necessarily. I think you'd have had time to phone 911, and if they'd gotten to you soon enough and pumped your stomachs . . ."

Listening to him was enough to make me feel like puking. Why had I eaten those cookies at Marie's? Chocolate tends to upset my stomach as it is.

"Obviously," Cyrus went on, "we need to discuss this."

"Obviously." My voice sounded hollow.

"Mom and I were just going to fix sandwiches," Roberta said, ignoring my piercing glare. "Toasted cheese. Why don't you have lunch with us and we can decide what to do."

What to do? My mind still wasn't functioning, that was plain to see. All I wanted was for Cyrus to go home and leave me alone to curl in a fetal position on my bed. Someone had tried to murder me? And Roberta? That's what really got to me. They hadn't cared who'd eaten the cookies. Whatever was going on, Roberta hadn't had anything to do with it. I must have, even if I didn't know what or how. Killing Roberta would have been a callous, misplaced deed.

The same thing could have happened at Marie's house, I realized suddenly. Who was to know that she wouldn't share the dish of lasagna? She must have had other people in the house at mealtime on several occasions following Lyle's death. Had she thrown away any other gift food she'd received and gently refused further contributions? I sincerely hoped so.

"That would be excellent," Cyrus said.

What would be? Oh, yes, Roberta had invited him to lunch. I certainly hadn't. I supposed we did need to have a discussion, but eating could have waited. Especially with those cookies making my stomach roil.

"You stay right there, Mom," Roberta said. "You look pale. I'll fix everything and you and Cyrus can begin."

"Thank you," I said weakly.

"First of all, who is going to the police?" Cyrus asked, settling his long frame on my couch.

"You are," I said firmly. "The less I have to do with them, the better as far as I'm concerned."

"They'll want to talk to you," he warned.

Again I had the feeling of being swept along, like being in a boat that had no oars in a fast current. With a large waterfall just around the next bend.

"Donna, why do I have the impression that I don't have your full attention?"

"Because you don't." I sighed. "I am totally flummoxed, discombobulated, disconcerted . . ."

"And a walking . . . no, seated . . . thesaurus. Pull yourself together. Surely you must have considered the possibility that these test results would show poison. Do you want to read the report?" He waved the envelope.

"No. I'll take your word for it. You can deliver it to the police. To Jake, of course. Chief Donniker would probably sneer and throw it in the wastebasket."

"Don't you think it would be politic to go to the top?"

"Maybe, but dangerous. At least we know it would get read if you contact Jake."

He shrugged. "Okay. Your decision. You're the one who'll have to take the consequences."

"Chief Donniker dislikes me as it is. He'll probably wish the poisoner had succeeded."

"Mom," Roberta said, sticking her head around the corner from the kitchen, "he isn't that bad."

"Worse," I said.

"It was the Chief who rescued me in the canoe that time," she pointed out. "Of course he chewed me out, but I deserved it."

"I'll give him that," I said. "I appreciate anyone who rescues my daughter. Okay, Chief Donniker it is."

"That isn't to say that we should count on him finding the murderer, poisoner, et al." Cyrus leaned back and stretched an arm along the back of the couch.

"Oh, definitely not."

"So," he said, "what do we do next?"

"Do? We? I appreciate your help, Cyrus. I really do. I'm sure I was ungracious in the shock of the moment. I'm quite glad that I am not dead, thanks to your intervention. But that doesn't mean that this is your problem."

"Why not?" he asked. "I told you I was bored. What better than to investigate a mystery? I would find it quite rewarding to solve the question before the police do and, incidentally, keep my entertaining next-door neighbor alive while I'm at it."

"I do believe that I can keep myself alive," I said. "I just wish I knew what I'd done to cause someone to want to poison me."

"More likely, what you know rather than what you've done. Let's face it, you may be tactless, a bit caustic at times and moved to action on impulse . . ."

"The slugs were quite well thought out, I assure you," I interrupted.

". . . but I sincerely doubt that you, yourself, have done anything to anyone that would make someone hate that much. You generally are quite respected." He sounded reluctant to make such an admission. "With a few exceptions, of course. You must have been an extraordinarily fine teacher."

"Exceptions?" I asked.

From the kitchen, I heard giggles. Then Roberta again appeared around the corner. "Lunch is ready," she said.

"Exceptions?" I asked again as I stood.

"Well, we all know about Chief Donniker. And there is that one woman . . ."

"Gloria Larson," I said. "I have never quite understood her animosity. My only real connection was when her daughter killed herself, and I couldn't have been more distressed and sympathetic. I also felt guilty, that somehow I should have been able to prevent the suicide, but that, of course, is unreasonable. A teacher can only do so much."

I pulled a chair out and sat down at the table, as Cyrus sat across from me where Roberta indicated. "Anyway," I went on, "Gloria became difficult toward everyone at that time. For a while, we all tended to forgive her, and then her actions clearly became habit and there was nothing anyone could do except put up with her. It's been so long now, though, that it seems unreasonable for her to hate the world. After all, many of those she's dealing with weren't even around at the time of Mary's death.''

"Well, let's change the subject while we eat," Roberta said. "Cyrus, tell me about yourself. Where are you from and how did you end up in Cedar Harbor?" She handed him a bowl of fruit salad that I had prepared that morning before we went to see Marie.

"By a circuitous route." He nodded his thanks and added a helping of the salad to the plate that held the golden brown sandwich. Roberta always did love toasted cheese and makes them to perfection, whereas I tend to become distracted and end up with a sandwich a mite too toasted.

"I grew up in Kansas and joined the Navy after college. I was stationed abroad a good deal of my career, but spent time in Bremerton many years ago and liked the country. My most recent assignment was in Washington, D.C., and I certainly didn't want to retire there. So, I thought about the various places I'd lived, remembered Puget Sound and came out to take a look."

"You had no desire to return to Kansas?" I asked.

"Have you ever spent a winter in Kansas?"

"But why Cedar Harbor specifically?" Roberta asked. "If I'm not being too personal."

"Not at all. I wasn't very scientific, I'm afraid. I allowed myself two months, rented a camper-van, and scouted the area. Both sides of the Sound, from Bellingham to Olympia and up to Sequim. When I drove into Cedar Harbor that day, it just felt right. And then when the real estate agent showed me the house and it was the size and price I was looking for, it seemed providential. I believe she was shocked when I wrote a check for earnest money after looking at the place for about twenty minutes. I did, of course, make it subject to an inspection."

Of course. Cyrus would. When I bought my house, I'd found the problem with the drain field only when the rains came that winter. The rotted boards under the leak in the kitchen pipes took longer.

"I wanted a complete change," he said. "No cities, not even old friends. I was just ready for a break and a new start."

"How sad," I said.

He shrugged and took a bite of sandwich. "I don't find it sad at all to make a new start. Sometimes you reach a point where it is the only choice. After my son died, of AIDS I'll say now so you won't find it necessary to wonder, and my wife left for more congenial company, I found it desirable to begin again."

What a story. Had Cyrus been unwilling to accept his son's problems and that led to the rift with his wife? It wouldn't be surprising for a military man. So macho, they all seem to be.

I thought he'd said all he intended to, but he surprised me by continuing. "She couldn't face," he said, looking at the refrigerator instead of us, "either his gayness nor his impending death. Enough said."

Poor man! Roberta met my eyes, and I knew she felt the same shock and sympathy that I did. Along with, on my part, guilt that I had so misjudged him. I wanted to apologize, but Roberta was sending waves toward me urging that I keep quiet. I'd seen that expression on her face all too often lately. I really must learn to temper my tongue. Cyrus had made it clear that he didn't want to talk about his past anymore and I couldn't blame him. Regardless of who did what, I was sorry for the entire family. What tragedy this virulent virus has wrought.

We were silent, then, until we finished eating the remaining small bits on our plates. Then Roberta led the way. "Let's adjourn to the living room," she said, picking up my plate as well as hers and setting them on the counter. "We can clean up later. I want to hear what you two think about what's going on. After all, I could have been poisoned, too, and I think it's my right to be included."

"Of course," Cyrus said. "I'm sure your mother will agree."

What made him so sure he knew how I felt about things?

Actually, I'd have liked to pack Roberta up and send her back to New York where she'd be safe. How ironic. We in this part of the country think of New York as one of the more dangerous places to live and our own as one of the safest.

Nevertheless, I knew Roberta would ignore me entirely if I suggested such a thing, and anyway, I didn't want to spoil the remaining short while she'd be here. Three thousand miles is too far to be separated from one's only child, and I wanted to take advantage of this unexpected visit, even though its cause had been unpleasant.

Roberta and I settled into chairs, with Cyrus again on the couch. Roberta reached into her purse and extracted a notebook and pen. "I want to make notes," she said. "A starting point. You two must have ideas about who hated Lyle Corrigan enough to kill him."

"Al Parry," I said.

"Marie Corrigan." Cyrus's voice boomed out simultaneously.

"What?" I asked. "Oh, come on. Marie is too meek and cowed. Besides, she was poisoned herself."

"Could have faked it," he insisted. "Easily. Remember, her dose was not lethal. And poison fits a woman with her personality better than Al. Can you really see him deciding to kill someone that way? Lots of noise and bluster, that's Al. Anyway, people don't usually go around killing over business matters."

"Maybe not, but people usually don't kill a partner they've been married to for . . . what did she say? Forty-two years?"

Roberta nodded. "That's a long time to live with a jerk. Still, look at all these battered women cases we've been reading about. Some tough old boy beats up on his wife and gets away with it and then something snaps and she does him in."

"Good point. I could certainly see Lyle as being . . . as having been a wife beater. Okay, put her on the list. I have to admit I suggested her to Jake initially, but later, when I analyzed her personality, I decided she was an unlikely candidate. But I think Al belongs on the list, too. There are undercurrents to him that make me nervous."

Cyrus agreed. "I didn't mean to eliminate him. But then, maybe we should include Mark Gasper. The two are connected, let's face it, and if Al is involved in something worth murdering over, say, massive bribery to county officials that could send both of them to jail, then Mark is, too."

"Granted. That reminds me. Did you ever do the snooping you intended concerning that?"

"*Mea culpa.* Put it out of mind entirely. I'll get on it right away."

That made me curious. "What exactly did you do in the Navy, Cyrus?" I asked. "You keep hinting that it wasn't exactly the usual guns and bad men routine."

"In a way it was," he said. "I'm an attorney, and I was in the office that investigates criminal misdeeds."

"I see." Roberta had been correct.

"All right," Roberta said, "three people so far. Anyone else?"

"Carrie Sanderson," I said reluctantly. "Lyle really did her dirt. But my gut feeling is that it can't be her. I'm not sure she even knew Jolene, and the girl certainly is connected somehow."

"Is she?" Roberta asked. "If so, maybe she really did kill Lyle. Lots of kids hate their fathers."

"She's a possibility, of course. I do wish Chief Donniker would get off his duff and find her. Put her on the list."

"Well," Roberta said, scribbling on her notepad. "I have a suggestion. Lyle, Junior. If we grant that Jolene could have hated her father, then so could he. After all, he's coming back and stepping in and taking over a prosperous business, which is an added motive, it seems to me."

"Good thinking," Cyrus said. "You're a fine member of this team."

"I can do better than that," Roberta suggested. "I used to know Lyle. I'll go today, and act as if I'm really glad to see him, and maybe I can renew . . ."

"Oh, no," I interrupted. "I don't want you involved."

"Involved? Just by getting together with the man and feeling out what sort of person he is?"

"Sounds good to me," Cyrus interjected.

"It's not your business," I snapped.

"Now, wait a minute," Roberta said. "If we're agreed that we're going to do some snooping, I want to be part of it. How can I sit here and do nothing and then go back to New York knowing some crazy out here might try to kill you again? I'm for action. Besides, what harm can come from my chatting with the man?"

"I wish I had more faith in the police," I said. "But, all right. I guess it wouldn't do any harm for you to renew your acquaintance with Will. You'd better call him that, by the way. For one thing," I suggested, "I wonder where he was living when his father died. For that matter, when his mother was poisoned. If he was in London or somewhere else far away, we could probably eliminate him."

"That should be easy to check on," she said. "What I'd like to do is find out more about his father. Lyle Corrigan's murder was the start of the whole thing. If we only knew why he was murdered, it should be easier to figure out who. Did you have the feeling that Mrs. Corrigan was lying about all that paperwork today? It didn't make sense to me that her son wasn't doing the job, if it was all concerning the hardware store that he's taking over."

"And one that he's had nothing to do with since he was a teenager. I agree, totally. If you can get any hints about the business—is it doing well, that sort of thing—it wouldn't hurt. But be careful, Roberta. I don't like your getting involved. Stay away from dark places."

She threw her head back and laughed. "If I have managed to survive dark places in New York, I can manage in Cedar Harbor. I carry an alarm in my purse that would blast the roof off a car, and a can of mace. I doubt I'll need them to handle Lyle William Corrigan. While Cyrus sees what he can find out about bribes and skullduggery, why don't you sound out your friend, Carrie? Maybe we can eliminate her, too."

"Good idea," Cyrus said. "If we can narrow the field, it ought to help."

"Yes," I agreed. "But there has to be a vital reason why Lyle was shot. And so far, we haven't touched on anything severe enough that appears to be a motive for that or for Jolene's disappearance."

"It's there," Cyrus said. "All we need to do is find it."

CHAPTER XV

Finding a police car in front of one's house first thing in the morning is guaranteed to start the day off on the wrong foot. Especially if that police car has been driven by our Billy. I drew open the drapes and groaned when I saw the now familiar vehicle parked dead center in front of my lot. The neighbors would all know whom he was here to call on.

I knew Chief Donniker had come and not Jake because he stood on the sidewalk, in full uniform, talking to Cyrus. When they saw me standing in the window, both men turned and faced me. No mistaking the subject of their conversation.

I yanked the cords to shut the curtains again, but the darn thing stuck halfway. Closing them wouldn't have done any good anyway, because the two men were already headed up the walk to my front door.

Thank goodness I had dressed before I came out from the bedroom for breakfast, I thought, glancing down at my black slacks and turquoise cotton shirt. I often don't, and that would have been embarrassing. I opened the door.

"Shush," I cautioned. "Roberta's still asleep. You're very early." I tried to admonish in a tone that would rouse memories of sixth grade for Billy. Maybe he'd respond as he'd been conditioned to do.

Unfortunately, my words had the opposite effect. Billy swelled, straightening to what must have been at least six-foot-two, and turned a purple hue that would worry me if I were his wife.

"Mrs. Galbreath," he said, "you have become a thorn in my side. You and—Mr. Bates, here. I thought I'd made it perfectly clear that you were to leave police matters to us."

"Cyrus took the report to you, didn't he? You did, didn't you, Cyrus?"

"I did." He nodded gravely. "Just as we agreed. May we come in?"

Since they'd already maneuvered themselves inside, his question seemed superfluous. "Please do. Let's go in the kitchen and I'll make coffee." I usually avoid the stuff, but this morning I thought it might be just the thing. It might also calm down the Chief if I served him cookies, too. I had a sudden impulse to take a lemon crisp from the freezer and add it to the plate just to see what happened, but I resisted.

"I don't quite see what you're angry about," I said as I drew water and filled the coffeemaker.

"In the first place," he said, "I don't appreciate your by-passing my department."

"Oh, but . . ." I began. A frown from Cyrus silenced me.

"Secondly, I want to know what you've been up to. Why did someone want to poison you? I mean, why did someone want to poison you enough to actually try?"

"Sit down, both of you," I ordered. "You make me nervous, hovering like that."

They sat. Cyrus looked perfectly relaxed, but the Chief perched rigidly on the edge of the chair. "What have you been up to?" he asked again.

"Nothing! I promise you. I have absolutely no idea why anyone has it in for me. I'd tell you if I did," I said, noting Roberta's sleepy-looking face peek around the corner from the hall, then disappear.

"I'm sure." The Chief was at his sarcastic best.

"I *would*. I have absolutely no desire to die. Which reminds me. Do you want the rest of the lemon-crisp cookies?"

"The rest? You mean you still have some?"

"In my freezer. Next to the raspberry jam I put up a couple of weeks ago."

He shut his eyes. "You have the lethal cookies next to your jam. Good thinking."

I shrugged. "What difference does it make? No one would be in my freezer besides me. And Roberta, of course. But she knows."

"Good morning, Chief Donniker," Roberta said, coming into the kitchen. Somehow she'd managed to dress and put on a touch of makeup in just those few minutes. She no longer looked sleepy. "How *nice* to see you." She held out her hand.

He scrambled to his feet as, lagging slightly, did Cyrus. "Roberta," Chief Donniker said, "good to see you, too. I thought I heard you lived in New York."

"I do. Just home for a visit. Seems like such a short while ago, Chief, when you rescued me in the canoe. Mom and I were just talking about that yesterday. I was so glad to see you, I remember."

"Just doing my duty." A smile touched the corners of his lips. Roberta had managed to make him feel good and defuse his ill-temper. She's skilled at that sort of thing, always has been. I guess she was forced to develop the talent because her mother tends to ruffle feathers with her frankness. Not that I cared, with Billy.

"You haven't changed a bit since," she flattered. "Coffee ready yet, Mom?"

"In just a minute."

"I suppose that you're here about those deadly cookies,"

she said. "Can you imagine? Someone tried to poison Mom and me?" Her dimple did its thing, and from then on, she had Billy eating out of her hand.

I'd have liked my breakfast while we talked, but coffee and cookies had to do unless I wanted to cook for the whole crowd. I didn't. "Someone must think I know more about Lyle's murder than I do," I suggested.

"I doubt that this present matter has anything to do with the killing," the Chief said. "That is, unless Jolene is hiding nearby. And I don't think that she can be. Our department would have found her by now."

"Oh, but . . . that would mean Jolene had tried to poison her own mother. *And* us," Roberta said, shocked.

Billy patted her hand in a gesture meant to be reassuring. "I don't think she did. She's responsible for the death of her father, but I don't believe this rash of poisonings has anything to do with the murder. We'll find, I'm sure, that something else is behind it. I repeat, Mrs. Galbreath, what have you been up to?" His gaze fixed on me as it would on an ant heading toward the crumbs of a picnic. Just before he squashed it.

"Absolutely nothing. Surely you can't mean that you think we have two murderers, actual and potential, in Cedar Harbor?"

"It looks that way, doesn't it?" His serious expression was meant to appear thoughtful, but merely came across as complacent.

Cyrus had been strangely quiet, his light eyes watching the proceedings as he took in everything that was said. He would be a formidable adversary, I decided. Perhaps it was just as well that he'd treated the slugs as a joke instead of retaliating.

The Chief showed no inclination to discuss possible suspects with us, so none of us volunteered an opinion to him. It wouldn't do any good. If we had any brilliant ideas, we still would need to work with Jake.

Finally, he drained the last of his coffee, picked up another of my oatmeal cookies and stood. "I'll take the rest of those you have stashed in your refrigerator," he said sternly. Roberta's mouth tightened, but she rose and retrieved them from the freezer. The garish box looked unpleasant now instead of innocent. I was just as glad to see it go.

"I assume," he said, "that this attempt on your life will finally convince you not to interfere with our investigation."

"Oh, absolutely." I crossed my fingers behind my back. Roberta saw my gesture, and she grinned at me quickly.

Billy noticed. He fixed a stern gaze on Roberta, and then on Cyrus. "That means all of you. *Stay out of my way.*"

"Just thought I was helping," Cyrus drawled. "Since I had a friend . . ."

"We have lab facilities available, too." He popped the oatmeal cookie in his mouth, then mumbled around it, "Thank you for the coffee and treats, Ma'am. Very good they were, too. I trust I won't need to call on you again."

"I trust so, too," I said as he departed with a definite swagger. For the benefit of the watching neighbors, no doubt. I managed to refrain from calling him Billy in retaliation for the "Ma'am." It was difficult. He brought out the worst in me.

"The man truly is an idiot," Cyrus said.

"Indeed."

"I assume we aren't going to pay any attention to him?"

"Absolutely not."

"Won't you have breakfast with Mom and me?" Roberta asked. "I'll fix pancakes."

"Please do," I agreed.

He blinked at me, but then said, "Thanks. I had a bowl of

corn flakes, but that was a long time ago, before I did my watering. Our morning, you know."

I didn't respond.

"It's going to be a nice day," he said.

I didn't think it was. When I'd been up early to go to the bathroom, I'd noticed the pink sky of a sunrise. In my experience, the old adage, "Red sun in the morning, sailors take warning," holds true. Still, I answered, "Glad to hear that."

Now he fixed his gaze on me. "Is something wrong?"

"Wrong? Why?"

"It's just that . . . aren't we being unusually agreeable this morning?"

"Agreeable? Aren't I always?"

Behind me, Roberta cracked up. "You two," she said through her laughter.

I supposed I did owe him an explanation. "It's just that . . . this is difficult to say, Cyrus, but Roberta had a little talk with me last evening, and I do believe she's right. I haven't shown the proper appreciation for what you did in our behalf. And perhaps I've been unnecessarily abrupt at times."

What she'd actually said was, "I don't mean to criticize, but have you *listened* to yourself? I've never seen you like this before. I hate to say it, but you two sound like a couple of kids squabbling."

Now I suggested, "Shall we start over? If we're going to work together on this little problem?"

"Sounds good to me." Cyrus held out his hand and I took it. We shook on our truce.

"I do appreciate being saved by your alertness," I said. "I *hope* I can be watchful enough to prevent a further episode. But it occurs to me that the person is unlikely to try poison again. It will be clear that I didn't get sick or die. The murderer—and I can't agree with the Chief that there are two different people—must know that I'm aware of the attack."

"I would think so," he said. "I don't know what to expect, but be vigilant."

"Maybe they don't know—yet," Roberta suggested. "You might have put the cookies in the freezer to serve later, the way Marie did."

"You're right. And I might have poisoned the whole neighborhood that way, even kids. What an incredibly irresponsible action." I was infuriated. "When you think of all the innocent people who might have died . . ."

"Just like terrorists," Cyrus said. "They don't care. Roberta's right. I suggest we don't tell anyone we've discovered the poison. Whoever it is will probably be content for a while, just waiting."

"But Chief Donniker . . ."

He nodded. "I know. I wonder if he has enough sense to keep it under his hat. Perhaps I can make a suggestion."

"Try Jake. Maybe he can funnel the suggestion into that pea brain. I don't suppose the police want another murder on their hands, even if the victim is me. Perhaps you can emphasize the possibility of innocent victims."

"Hotcakes coming up," Roberta sang out. What a joy that girl is. I'm a lucky woman.

While we ate, I thought back to the rest of the conversation she and I had had over our evening tea. "Cyrus is such a nice man," she'd said. "I don't see why he irritates you so. I wonder . . . he kind of reminds me of Dad."

"Don't be *silly*," I'd exploded. "You take after your father. He was laid back, gentle, intelligent . . ."

"Uh, huh," Roberta interrupted. "And he also ruled the roost."

"Oh, come on, you barely remember him."

"Yes, but you've told me stories. How he decided you'd quit college and have me."

"We decided that together."

"That's not the way I remember hearing it," she'd said. "I think Cyrus even looks a little like Dad."

"Your father had dark hair, like yours."

"It's the bearing, maybe. Tall, confident. But there's something about his nose . . ."

"Humph."

"Besides, I suspect Cyrus *is* laid back and gentle, and it's obvious he's intelligent."

"You're being totally ridiculous," I'd said. "Although, you're right about my behavior, I'm sorry to admit. I still resent the way he put up that fence, but I guess I can forgive him that, all things considered. You're like your father, anyway. I was always the volatile one, and you and he would look at me with brown eyes that were exactly alike, and I'd . . ." I swallowed. Even after all these years, I missed Bob.

"Donna," Cyrus said suddenly, snapping me out of my remembrances and bringing me back to the present. A present that included Cyrus sharing our breakfast table.

"Hum, yes?"

"I wasn't asking a question, I was just meditating." He slathered margarine on his second stack of pancakes. "Short for what? Madonna?"

"Mother's name is Madonna Rose. Isn't that lovely?" For once Roberta did not show discretion. Didn't she remember how much I hated my name?

"Lovely," Cyrus said. "Suits you."

"Oh, come on. I have never understood what came over my parents in choosing it. Surely they must have seen even as they held me for the first time that I'd never live up to it? I prefer practical names such as Roberta."

Roberta had the grace to look embarrassed. "Sorry. I forgot that you don't like to use it."

"It fits a woman who grows exquisite flowers," Cyrus said, forking up a bite. He waved it in mid-air. The little bit of pancake didn't have the nerve to fall off. "If you don't like Madonna, though, I shall ignore my knowledge. However . . . Donna Rose," he said triumphantly. "I'll call you Donna Rose. That's perfect. It fits you to a T." He finished the delivery of the food, chewing and swallowing while I thought.

Truce or no truce, I didn't want to egg this man on. He was quite capable of calling me Madonna in public, a name I had never cared for and one I liked even less now that that dreadful rock singer was baring herself in public. If I stayed quiet on the subject, perhaps he'd forget all about it.

"Well, let's get started," Roberta said. "I plan to drop into the hardware store this morning. Is there something you need, Mom?"

"Oh, I don't know. How about a couple of paint brushes? I can always use them. And a roll of masking tape."

"Okay. I thought if I timed it right, I might wangle an invitation to lunch."

"And I shall begin snooping by going to the County Courthouse," Cyrus said.

"Okay. I'll give Carrie a call and see if we can't get together. I'll think of some excuse."

Cyrus left shortly after, and I cleaned up the dishes while Roberta put in a load of laundry. I was just thinking of what I'd say to Carrie when the doorbell rang. As I walked to the door to answer, I could see a police car in front again. What now?

Girding myself to be polite no matter what, I opened the door. Instead of the Chief as I feared, Jake stood there. What a relief, I thought, as I invited him in.

"Mrs. Galbreath," he asked. "Can you tell me why your fingerprints are all over the library books about plant poisons?"

CHAPTER XVI

"You can't possibly suspect my mother!" Roberta had heard
Jake arrive and, steaming, burst out of her bedroom.

I got my voice back and introduced them. "My daughter,
Roberta Schwartz. And this is Jake Santorini," I told her.
"You've heard us mention him."

"Indeed I have," she said. "The hope of the Cedar Harbor
Police Department. The one who's supposed to be intelligent. Intelligent enough, I would assume, to realize that my
mother never shot anyone, nor poisoned, nor . . ." Her face
was turning red. This, the daughter that I had always thought
of as phlegmatic?

"I suggest you calm down," Jake said, with a hint of a
smile. "You might listen to what I have to say."

"Surely all you had to do was ask the librarian when I
checked those books out," I said.

"Easier said than done. The right to privacy, you know."

"Privacy?" Roberta asked. "What's private about checking fingerprints of everyone who's taken out a book? Are you
checking also, to see who's read *Sex*?"

"Couldn't," Jake said calmly. "Our library didn't buy it."

Jake wasn't acting as though he'd come to arrest me, I decided. Not yet, anyway. "Come in and sit down," I suggested,
"and explain what this is all about."

"It's an explanation from you I need," he said, but he settled down in a leisurely manner in my Swedish leather chair.

I perched on the couch, but Roberta remained standing, obviously still mistrusting Jake. "Simple enough," I said. "I was curious. I knew, vaguely, that plants in all our yards could be poisonous, but I didn't know details. If you'd seen the looks on people's faces at the Historical Society meeting when Will Corrigan announced what had poisoned Marie, you'd have been curious, too."

"Sounds reasonable . . . to me," he said.

"But not to the Chief."

"He doesn't know about it yet. It was my idea to check."

"I see. Did you find any other useful prints?" I asked.

He glanced at me obliquely, but didn't answer.

I sighed. "I know. Police secrets."

"Well, you can't really expect me to tell you all our business."

"Especially since I'm obviously a suspect."

Now his expression sharpened. "In my book, a murderer needs a motive, not just the knowledge of how to do it."

Roberta sat down now, but her back straightened when he went on, "Of course, should we find some reason that Lyle's death benefited you in any way . . ."

"Nonsense." Roberta's voice showed her anger.

Jake leaned forward, which wasn't easy in that chair, and shrugged. "Chief Donniker can make life unpleasant, should he fix on you as a suspect."

"That would be foolish," Roberta said. "Even I know he needs some evidence, and he's not going to find it."

"Chief Donniker *is* foolish."

I was surprised. "You've never admitted it before."

"I can't exactly go around criticizing my boss," he said, "and keep my job."

"Then why are you telling us?"

"Because you're in danger of muddying the waters. I intend to solve this case." His expression became stern. "I'm going to find out who the murderer is, and along the way, I'm going to show up the Chief for being the inadequate bungler that he is, and I am going to take his job away from him." He leaned back now, a watchful expression in his eyes.

"And if my comments leave this room," he continued in a deceptively mild tone, "*I* shall personally make life unpleasant for you. Beginning with, did you realize that the tabs on your car license are outdated? I noticed the other day. You'd better do something about it."

"Oh." I was nonplussed. "If they just didn't send that darn form so far ahead. I hate to pay the government any earlier than necessary, but I did forget. Thank you."

"You also have a taillight out. I spotted that a couple of days ago when we had that fog."

"Mom," Roberta said, "you told me about that. Haven't you fixed it yet?"

"No, of course not," I snapped. "I've been too busy."

"Too busy interfering with the police?" he asked.

"Too busy with unnecessary interviews with the police . . . No, I really don't have an excuse, Jake. Thanks again, and I'll get it fixed right away."

Smiling, he said, "For the record, just kidding about the book. Thought I'd see your reaction."

"Jake! How could you! How . . ."

He interrupted, holding up a hand. "Now I'd like to ask, and please tell me the truth, has anything unusual happened concerning any of the people you know who might be involved in this case?"

Roberta's gaze met mine. Should we tell him how we were proceeding? Surely not. We didn't *know* anything yet. Neither Roberta's plan to approach Will nor my impending conversation with Carrie was anything but a fishing expedition.

Cyrus was snooping, but only hoping to find something peculiar enough to follow up on. So far we didn't have anything to go on. No out-of-character behavior from anyone.

Except, I remembered suddenly, Sue's turnabout concerning the water board. Jake and she apparently had a thing going. He'd be in a better position than I to find out what she was up to. If it was an innocent decision, he might know already.

"There is one thing," I said. "Sue Reilly. She's decided she's willing to be on the water board."

"So?"

"So she told me unequivocally that she would not, could not, because of babysitting expense. And now she has changed her mind. And I had a sudden suspicion . . ." Oh-oh. Now I was in a pickle. How was I going to say that I wondered if Sue had begun to see Mark Gasper, and was being influenced by him? What if my meddling ruined a perfectly good relationship between Jake and Sue? I did seem to be tromping on a lot of toes these days.

Jake looked at me sternly. "Now you're doing exactly what I've been complaining about. You know something and you won't tell me and you think you'll check on it yourself. Right?"

"No, no," I protested, "it's just that . . ."

Roberta didn't have my compunction, not surprising since she had barely met Jake, *and* under circumstances that raised her ire, and she'd never met Sue. "What Mom is trying to say is that she thinks Susan Reilly might be hanging around with this Mark Gasper person."

"Oh, but she . . . Jake . . ."

Jake stood up. "Sue Reilly is a very nice, intelligent woman," he said. "Pretty, too." A flash of regret crossed his face. "But she's bright enough to see that Mark Gasper has a

155

lot more money than any cop ever will have. If you're worried that you were telling me something I didn't know, you don't need to. But I don't think what Sue does with her personal life has any bearing on the case. I remember you pointed out that Gasper benefited from Lyle's death, and we're investigating, I assure you. What Sue does now will have no effect on the case. And her love life is her own business."

He said the last so firmly that I didn't dare argue, but I didn't agree. Her relationship with Mark—and with the water board—*was* our business, if nothing else because it potentially affected our community. I still wasn't sure what I thought about Shadybrook Meadows, but I did know that I wanted any decision made by our board to be based on thoughtful analysis and a consensus, if possible. I didn't want it to be made because of underhanded activities. That included bribes paid to Al Parry or romancing done to Sue. Would Mark Gasper be cynical enough to pay suit to a comely widow only to further his own position?

I didn't know the man well enough to decide. Perhaps becoming better acquainted with him was on the agenda.

Jake departed then, leaving me with a lot to think about.

While we conducted our separate investigations, life had to go on, of course. There was the usual cleaning, shopping and cooking, and Roberta visited old friends. The garden didn't need as much weeding at this time of year, but sprinkling became even more imperative. In view of our recent collaboration, I tried to avoid irritating Cyrus, although I felt sneaky, peering through the fence, checking his driveway for his red sports vehicle, before watering that wasn't on "our" day. I needed to get used to sneaky, though, if I was going to succeed as a detective. I was always very aware that the days were counting down until Roberta had to return to New York.

I had to take time off to attend a funeral, which was frustrating, but people don't die according to schedule. Funerals are barbaric customs, in my opinion, and I avoid them whenever possible. But when a long-standing friend chooses to arrange one to honor her husband, a person feels obligated to attend.

Meg Chisholm and I had grown up together. We were the best of friends: I, the leader and she the follower. That may not sound the best mix for friendship, but for us it led to remarkably stress-free formative years. We had not seen as much of each other in the last couple of decades, however. Perhaps inevitably, our paths diverged with our marriages. She became quite the social hostess and committee member, not my forte at all, even had I not been forced, in a relatively short time, to concentrate on becoming educated and earning a living.

I always wondered whether that sort of life was what Meg really wanted, to be a satellite for her very successful husband, but she was a loyal wife and never discussed it. Now that Fred was dead, having collapsed of a massive heart attack while playing golf, I wondered what would happen to Meg.

There was no real opportunity to talk to her at the funeral or the gathering afterwards, a traditional affair attended by huge numbers of people, so I returned home vaguely dissatisfied and vowing to make more effort to get together with Meg now that we were both widows.

Roberta made progress in renewing her scant friendship with Will. He'd been away long enough that he had no close friends in town, and he seemed to welcome her attention. Roberta, too, surprisingly, was enjoying the association. I felt that she was answering a need after what was apparently an extended period of her husband's lack of interest, but she insisted that that wasn't so. She enjoyed Will, she said; he was nice. Which, if true, was remarkable considering his family. I had to admit that he'd given me that impression the few times I'd seen him since he'd returned to town.

My investigating, though, had been unsatisfactory so far. Well, not totally. While my questioning led me no closer to the murderer, I did manage to eliminate Carrie as a suspect, in Lyle's murder at least. In my own mind, if not Chief Donniker's, that also eliminated her from being a suspect for the other nefarious doings, since there was no doubt to anyone of normal intelligence that the murder and poisonings were connected. Roberta and Cyrus agreed with me.

It had been so simple to find out, once I asked the right question. I spent the better part of a morning turning over rocks and wallowing in holes on the tide flats to reach the point of making that crucial query.

I'd called Carrie to suggest we get together. "We don't see enough of each other," I said. "Do you have plans for tomorrow?"

"Only that great tide," she'd answered. "Didn't you notice? It's the lowest this year, almost a minus four."

"Oh, no. How'd I miss that?" I truly do like to go for clams when nature evens the odds. It was a measure of how distracted I'd become that I hadn't paid attention to the tide tables. Usually the morning paper informs us when there is to be an especially low one, but I just hadn't had time lately to read the paper thoroughly. "Let's go. I mean, if you don't mind my horning in."

"Of course not. I'd love company. Although, as you know, half the county will be out there with us. Will Roberta want to go, too?"

"I'll check." We set a time and said goodbye.

I'd asked Roberta. "Are you kidding?" She glanced at her hands. "The last time I went, it took my fingernails weeks to recover. I'll take a bye. I'll enjoy eating them, though."

I made a face at her and she laughed. "Anyway, duty calls. I promised to meet Will for coffee at the bakery this morning."

"Perhaps it's just as well," I admitted. "Carrie's more likely to open up to me without you being there, I would think. Two old widows having a heart-to-heart."

"Hah. You make it sound like a couple of doddering women reminiscing over tea."

"Not quite. I trust I'll never reach that state. Nor Carrie. If we live that long, I'll still be puttering in the garden in an old straw hat and Carrie will be sweeping into the opera wearing the latest gown and with jewels on her ears."

"Will she have the money?"

"I don't know. She dresses well, but occasionally makes references that indicate money is tight."

Predictably, our choices of attire for clam digging were poles apart. I always wear my shabbiest jeans and my oldest sweatshirt, the red one that faded so badly. It had also continued shrinking a bit every time it was washed, as they are wont to do, until its sleeves left my wrists exposed as well as my hands. That was all right. I'd need to shove the sleeves up out of the way, regardless.

Carrie, however, wore stylish pants that came just below her knees, the sort we actually called clam diggers when we were young, a crisp green-checked gingham blouse and a windbreaker of the same shade. A visored cap sat jauntily on her white curls. Our styles of chasing clams were equally different, although I knew that from previous expeditions with her. She uses a short-handled clam shovel. I prefer to get right down on the sand and dig with my hands. Clams can be so elusive, and my method is usually much more successful.

It was today. I counted through the clams in my bucket. "Thirty-nine, forty, my limit," then sat back on my haunches and glanced down ruefully at myself. I was wet, sticky and sandy. Carrie, on the other hand, was unruffled other than having folded back the sleeves of her jacket and acquiring one sandy smudge on her pants.

I glanced in her half-full bucket. "I'll help."

"Nah," she answered. "I'll get just a few more and that'll be enough for me. I love butter clams once in a while, but then I'm satisfied."

"But you could make chowder . . ."

She shook her head. "Never do. It's too much trouble just for me." She stuck her shovel in the gravelly sand as she spoke.

So far we hadn't had a chance for any real talking and we hadn't touched on the murder at all. I gazed out at the gently lapping water, today gray and white because the overcast had not yet burned off. How was I going to tactfully bring up the subject of Carrie's possible complicity in crime? I should have thought out what I was going to say more thoroughly. It wasn't the first time I'd leaped into a situation before thinking it through.

Carrie leaned on her shovel and looked at me, an expression of commiseration on her face. "You're thinking of Lyle, aren't you? I'm sorry. I never thought, when I suggested coming here, that this was nearby to where you . . ."

"Yes, I guess I was thinking of him, of everything that's been happening." I had been, true, but not quite in the way she was envisioning. She was right about the location, though. His body had been lying not that far away. I had thought about the event as we'd headed down the stairs to the beach, but then I'd resolutely put it out of my mind. Lyle was gone. Nothing would change that. But the murderer was still undiscovered and was not, it appeared, finished.

Since I had been the most recent target for vengeance, I had a vested interest in seeing the murderer unmasked and solving the mystery of what had happened to Jolene. But still, what was I going to say to find out if Carrie could possibly be the murderer without sounding accusing? It was more difficult than it might have been because basically I was convinced that Carrie was innocent. I'd known her a good many years and I was sure she didn't have it in her, both from the standpoint of wanting to kill someone, and also having the guts to do so.

"I was thinking of Marie," I finally said, and Carrie went back to her shoveling. "Of how hard this has all been on her."

"Yes, I suppose so." She turned over a shovelful of grit and poked around gently. One clam. She dropped it in her bucket.

"Roberta and I called on her last week," I went on. "She was busy going through Lyle's papers. We all do collect so many, and I suppose it's even worse when you're running a business."

"I know," she said. "I still have a box or two left. I had to take care of all the ones dealing with taxes, of course."

"Um. Well, Marie was just finishing that day. Said she'd gone through everything and was relieved to be done."

"Good for her. It was therapy, I suppose, in a way."

Carrie didn't sound interested in the question of Marie's papers, one way or another. I tried another tack. "I had to go to a funeral the other day, the husband of an old friend, and it was enormous. It made me wonder. I suppose a lot of people showed up for Lyle's, his being in business and all. I didn't feel obligated to go just because I found his body."

"Well, *I* certainly wouldn't have attended, either, feeling the way I did about him. I wasn't here that week, though. That's when I went to California to visit my college roommate. Remember my telling you I was going?"

"So you did." A rush of good feeling washed over me. Carrie hadn't been here at all when Lyle was murdered. I'd known in my heart she hadn't done it, but I felt even better that there was proof. "Did you have a wonderful time?" I asked.

The three of us, Roberta, Cyrus and I, gathered that evening to compare notes. Cyrus suggested, even insisted, that we come to his house. "You've never been inside," he'd said. "I'd be honored."

"Well, if you put it that way . . ."

I wondered what to expect in the way of décor. "Probably austere," I warned Roberta as we cut across the lawn to his front walk. "Like him. Neat. Plain."

"Um, we'll see," Roberta answered. "I think you're misjudging Cyrus when you think of him as plain." I knew she had a somewhat different picture of him than I did, but she hadn't had to deal with the man one solid year as I had.

His house was basically the same design as mine. Typical tract house except for being on a larger lot than some. An L-shaped living room and eating area, with traffic patterns coming in a central front door and diverging toward the bedrooms or along the edge of the living room to reach the kitchen. There all resemblance stopped.

It was my living room that appeared austere in comparison. I have always believed, not in austerity, but in being functional. I have never wanted to spend the time to dust a covey of small objects. My first reaction, as I stepped in the door, was to wonder who *did* dust his collections.

Because collections he had. As I stood and stared, my first thought was that the room resembled a museum. There was a hideous mask—no, a mask with a hideous expression but otherwise admirable—that, guessing, probably came from New Guinea or at least that part of the world. On each side were mounted war-like Stone Age implements. The rock lashed to an intricately carved handle could, I suppose, have been used to pound, but my guess was that the intent was to pound heads rather than wooden beams.

"Magnificent," Roberta said, standing in front of a framed exotic-looking print.

Over the fireplace was a collection of guns: a long-barreled rifle with powder horn, a couple that looked as if pirates might have carried them. Everywhere I looked, tables and walls were covered with other intriguing items. "I hope you have insurance," I said, shaking myself out of my reverie.

"Of course." He sounded surprised at my question. "And a very good system of security."

"Um, you must have been gathering mementos as you traveled."

He shrugged. "Come on back," he suggested. "I've made dessert."

Roberta's eyes caught mine. Hers were plainly suggesting that I not say we'd already had some. Plain gingersnaps, but dessert nevertheless. Well, I supposed she was right, given that I was trying to avoid irritating Cyrus. It really was an unexpected gesture on his part. As we settled around his table, a modern contraption of glass and metal, he reached into his refrigerator and removed tall sherbet glasses with a frothy concoction. "Raspberry sorbet," he said. "My own raspberries, of course."

"Of course."

"May I help?" Roberta offered.

"Yes, thanks. I have hot water, a choice of tea bags and coffee. If you'd like to fix your own and your mom's . . ."

She bounced up, and in a few moments we were all taken care of and eating the sorbet. It was delicious, I had to admit. Still, it was time to get to what we were here for. "Are you having any luck at the county offices?" I asked.

"Actually, I am. I'm on the track of something, I think, but I'd rather not talk about it until I'm sure."

"Oh, come on. Brainstorming is what we're here for."

He smiled and ignored me, taking a sip of coffee.

"Oh, very well. I did make progress of a sort. We can completely eliminate Carrie," I explained.

"Good," Cyrus said. "We can cross her off the list. How are you coming with Will?" he asked Roberta. "Is he as innocent as he gives the impression of being?"

"My gut feeling is that he is," she answered. "Although, I found out one thing. You remember all those papers of Lyle's? Marie was right. Someone had gone through them. Will. But he doesn't want her to know. There was something in them that he wouldn't discuss."

"You didn't tell me that," I said.

"Just hadn't gotten to it," she answered. "You were so busy looking at the scrapbook of Jolene's."

"What scrapbook?" Cyrus's tone was sharp.

"Oh, nothing important about the murder," I assured him. "This dated from about the time she was a student of mine. In fact, there were school papers . . . It's a sad collection, really, because there was so little that was joyous in it.

She seems to have collected menus, for instance, but there was always a notation, and they were inevitably from times she had been out to dinner with her parents. It doesn't strike me that the most exciting event in a young girl's life should be such an occasion."

"Will sent it because he thought Mom would appreciate some of the comments she'd made about school. After one paper, she'd scribbled, 'Best year I've had.' "

"Well, she might have been referring to the fact that she'd made a friend that year. There were several references to poor Mary. I didn't have time to finish going through it. I brought it," I reached to the floor where I'd laid the faded book and produced it, "but just so you could get a feeling for her. We're not going to solve a murder with a schoolgirl's old scrapbook." I handed it to him, and he began to leaf through it.

"I wonder if she stopped it when Mary died," he said, turning to the back.

"I wonder—I hadn't thought of that." I leaned forward, and he tipped the book sideways to that I could look, too.

"Oh, I remember that paper," I said. "It was the best thing she ever wrote. I really thought that she might be developing some writing talent."

It was the last page that had anything pasted or written on it, Cyrus determined quickly, flipping through the remaining blank ones.

"Let me see that again," I said. "I remember now, she wrote that shortly after Mary shot herself. It was about friendship, as I recall." He pushed the book over so that I could read the page without straining my neck.

I scanned the page quickly, and tears formed in my eyes. It was well written for a twelve-year-old and it was sad. I was right. It referred, in an oblique fashion, to her friendship with

Mary and Mary's death. It also, I saw, made another reference. One that I had forgotten and one that could be crucial.

Wiping my eyes as I held my finger to the spot, I announced, "I think I've just discovered something important."

CHAPTER XVII

"What? What?" Cyrus leaned forward to read where I was pointing. "That memory of yours . . ."

"A place," I said. "One that was important to both girls."

"Read it aloud, Mom, would you?" Roberta asked.

I took the scrapbook from Cyrus. "I'll skip to the pertinent part," I said, "although you'll want to read the whole essay to get a picture of the girl Jolene was. And I'm very much afraid that 'was' is the operative word, not that I have any real hopes that she could still be alive."

"Quit dangling us in suspense," Cyrus said.

"Oh, very well. Here's what she wrote: 'A place for friends, a golden place, where only two found happiness. Quiet, just us, alone with our sadness, and now there is only one. One with memories, to bear the grief without comfort. Why did you leave me, my only friend?' "

We were silent for a moment, and then Cyrus asked quietly, "You know where this is located?"

"But—just because she and Mary shared a—a particular spot, what makes you think . . ." Roberta was not being as coherent as she usually is.

"That we might find her body there? I'm not sure, of course, but it would be a reasonable place to look. If a disturbed young woman did decide to do away with herself, much as I hate to consider the possibility since it would probably indicate that she had also killed her father, what better place than the one where her long dead friend shot herself?"

"And you do know where it is," Cyrus stated baldly.

"Even I know," Roberta said, "or at least the general vicinity. I remember now, that Mary's body was found there and that she'd left a note. I only recall dimly, but wasn't the note something like this essay? Talking about a secret place between friends?"

I nodded. "Mary's father, as I recollect, knew where their refuge was."

"And where is it?" Cyrus asked, a look of reluctant patience on his face.

"It's a pocket beach," I said. "No, actually, more of a cave, as I recall it being described. One of those spots that any child would think was a sanctuary."

"I used to love anywhere on the beach that the driftwood piled up and made a hideout," Roberta said. "I didn't have anything to hide from, but I still loved the feeling."

"This one," I explained to Cyrus, "is at the base of a high cliff, that one north of town. It's a place where rocky ledges make it difficult to beach a boat at high tide. At low, long tide flats make it equally difficult. I'm not sure how the girls ever found the place, if anyone knew."

"We'll want to go look half-way between high and low tides, I assume?"

"You agree we should then, Cyrus?"

"What about your tame policeman, Mom? Aren't you going to tell him?"

"Oh, I don't think so. I mean—that miserable Chief Donniker. He always makes things so difficult. Can you imagine his derision if I'm wrong? It *is* in the nature of a hunch, after all."

"I don't imagine he'll be happy with us if you're right, either, for investigating on our own—if that bothers you," Cyrus commented.

I felt a grim smile spread on my face. "Unfortunately, if we're right, very likely it makes him right about Jolene, also. I doubt if we'd hear much from the Chief except, 'I told you so.' "

"I wonder . . ." Roberta said musingly. "Shouldn't we ask Will if he wants to go? He'd have more at stake than anyone, except his mother, of course, and I don't think it would be a good idea to include her. Do you know exactly where it is? Have you ever been there?"

"No, I haven't. For me, it was a place to avoid, not to search out."

"Will ought to know. Besides, he has one thing we don't."

"What's that?" Cyrus asked.

"A boat."

Will wanted to leave immediately when Roberta called him. She pointed out that darkness would fall before we could possibly go and return, and furthermore that the tide wasn't right. He reluctantly agreed to wait until noon the next day, saying that he could arrange for a part-time employee to cover for him at the store. His mother, fortunately, was entertaining a guest in the living room and was unable to hear him because he and Roberta both agreed that it wouldn't do to alarm Marie unless it became necessary.

So, the next day, we met him at the community boat launch, where we were forced to wait in line for our turn, something we hadn't anticipated. Thus, we set out in his very nice inboard motorboat at about one o'clock. He'd done something very practical—brought a small, inflated dinghy, which he suspended behind us on a rope. It bounced merrily in our wake like a large, peculiarly-shaped red balloon.

"It might be easier to go ashore in this," he'd explained. He did know the exact location of Mary and Jolene's secret hideaway. "I followed them once," he said. "My mother asked me to. She wondered where they were going and what they were up to. I don't know why someone didn't think of looking there."

I pointed out that even Chief Donniker had not been on the scene twenty-three years ago. As I recall, he'd started as a policeman in some small town up in the mountains. They, no doubt, had been glad to see his rear end when he departed. Probably one of those situations where they gave him a good recommendation to get rid of him.

"Mother should have thought of it," Will said.

"But your mother probably never has accepted the Chief's premise that Jolene killed your father."

"No. Of course not. To tell the truth, I'm not prepared to accept that explanation myself." He turned the steering wheel so that we met the wake of a passing boat head-on. We still lurched unpleasantly. I never did see the appeal of small speedboats.

Being out on the water, however, on a day such as this would have been extremely pleasant had our journey not had such a macabre purpose. The sky and the water were both that intense blue of a perfect summer day. Boats in the channel had sails of every hue, and the mountains beyond, though becoming mostly bare as they do each August, rose in jagged splendor. Roberta was sunning herself on the prow, and Cyrus and I sat in the rear as Will steered.

"What do you think has happened to your sister?" Cyrus asked. He was dressed as if boating were an everyday occurrence for him. He wore light blue denim pants, a zippered dark blue jacket that somehow had a nautical appearance, and blue and white deck shoes. One of those visored caps with gold braid was set firmly on his head.

I tried desperately to corral my hair, as I wished I'd thought to wear a cap or scarf. Obviously, my mind did not want to focus on Jolene and what we might find at our destination. It was the fault of the day, I think. It wasn't meant for uncovering dark secrets.

Nevertheless, I forced myself to listen with half an ear. "I haven't lived with her for a long time," Will said, not really answering Cyrus's question, "and people change. But Jolene was—nice. I never did see why she couldn't seem to make friends. She was shy, but lots of shy people have friends."

"Then you don't think we'll find anything today?" Cyrus asked.

"I didn't say that." He rubbed a hand through his hair, which didn't dishevel it any more than it had been already. "It just feels right, somehow, since no one has found any trace of her. No trail. No charge cards have been used. No one has seen her. I'll give the Chief credit. He did try to find her. The way people say she looks now—someone would have noticed her and remembered her if she'd been on a bus or train. Her car was still parked behind the Satterburg cottage, you know."

"In all that time you were away, didn't she ever try to get in touch with you, or you with her?" It seemed odd to me if neither of them had, since he sounded as if he was fond of his sister.

He sighed. "At first, when I took off, I didn't want anything to do with any of them. Jolene was younger, of course, and it would have been impossible for her to get away to meet me. Then, later, I did try. By then it was too late, and even my mother didn't know where she was."

What a pitiful family, it occurred to me. "What did you do

all those years?" I asked quietly. "Unless you don't want to talk about it."

"I don't mind," he said. "I bummed around for a while, job to job, but then I realized that I didn't want to spend the rest of my life like that. I seemed to remember a certain teacher who kept urging me to go to college . . ." He grinned at me, and with that smile I could see what about him appealed to Roberta even if, so far, she'd only admitted to being a friend. "Anyway, I started in a community college, and ended up getting my degree in business at the U of Oregon. I've got a good job, Mrs. G. I'm the controller for a small company in Portland. They've granted me a leave until I get things straightened out."

"You're going back then?" I found I was obscurely disappointed.

"I'm not sure. I'll decide when everything's resolved."

The level of the land beside us had been slowly ascending as we moved northward. "Aren't we almost there?" I asked, looking at the whitish-colored bluff that rose several hundred feet.

"Yes." Will slowed the motor and turned the wheel to the right. We moved deliberately toward the shore, accompanied only by the blub-blub sound of the water behind the boat. The growing tension was palpable, and no one spoke. Finally Will cut the motor entirely.

"Watch for the rock ledge," he called to Roberta. "Let me know as soon as you see it."

"Okay," she answered, leaning intently over the water. The boat drifted in the direction we'd been heading. I could see where Will wanted to go. At the base of the cliff was a small patch of greenery, either stunted trees or vine maples. Elsewhere along this stretch of land, the water lapped against the bluff itself.

"Now," she called, "but it's down several feet."

"That's okay," he answered, "I'd rather row than take a chance on hitting a rock. Cyrus, take care of the anchor, will you?"

Cyrus nodded, and tossed it overboard.

I took a deep breath, suddenly reluctant to find out if the answer lay here. Specifically, I was reluctant to find out if Jolene's body lay here.

I'm a very pragmatic person, not given to impulses and urges. I've never felt that I was one of those fortunate—or unfortunate—souls who are endowed with extrasensory perception. Why, now, did I feel pulled toward that small beach, where I could see a few large logs that had drifted in and formed their usual pattern? If there was a cave there, I couldn't see it.

I pulled myself together, to see that Cyrus had hauled the dinghy forward and was picking up oars. I rose, but he shook his head and held up a hand in restraint. "I'm going alone."

Will stood beside me, his mouth open. I noticed he was pale under his tan. Roberta scrambled alongside the cabin and approached.

"But . . ." I began.

Cyrus maneuvered himself over the edge into the unstable-looking red boat. "Have any of you ever seen a corpse, outside of a funeral home?"

No one answered, although a vision of Lyle's unfortunate body flashed into my mind. Cyrus had forgotten. I wanted to. I wouldn't argue.

"I have. If there's anything there to discover, I'll do it. Wait here."

Will's mouth shut, but he didn't argue either. I couldn't blame him. It would be especially bad should her body be here, for him, her brother. Cyrus was being unexpectedly, and correctly, sensitive. We could wait. No one said anything as he inserted the oars into the oarlocks and pushed the dinghy away. We watched in silence as he rowed toward the shore.

It seemed hellishly long as we waited. None of us had anything to say. I could only think about the girl Jolene had been, with the potential of the young, the girl she'd become, strange but alive, and still, presumably, with that potential. I thought about her father, with all his meanness, and wondered what had happened to him, in turn, to make him the unpleasant person he'd become. Was there ever a stop to it? Would Will—had Will been able to break the chain that descended through God knew how many generations?

And then I thought about the murder. If Jolene's body did lie here, then I feared that Chief Donniker would have been proved correct, that she had killed her father and then, in remorse perhaps, herself. But that just didn't feel right. Because then, of course, who had tried to poison Marie and me?

Cyrus reached the shore and scrambled onto a silvered log, tying the dinghy to an extended branch. He then pushed through some green shrubbery and disappeared. I think we were all holding our breath.

He wasn't gone long. Someone let that breath out in a sigh. He was returning, too quickly. Cyrus untied the boat and climbed in. We watched as he rowed toward us, fast.

He reached us and tossed the end of the rope to Will, who raised his eyebrows questioningly. Cyrus nodded. "Let's call Jake. She's there." He pulled a cell phone from his pocket.

CHAPTER XVIII

Chief Donniker was elated. He was sure that finding Jolene's body proved that his theories were right. The buttons on his shirt were in danger of popping off, he was bursting so with pride. He couldn't have been more patronizing. "If you amateur so-called detectives would just leave it to the professionals . . ."

I'm afraid I snorted. Roberta kicked me in the ankle, and I said, "Ouch," instead of what I intended. Which was, of course, that the body would still be lying on the beach if it hadn't been for us.

His office was crowded. We had extracted a promise from Jake to let us know what the official findings were after the police and the coroner completed their investigation at the site. So now, Roberta and I were seated in the small room and Cyrus and Will flanked us, standing. Jake stood in the corner behind the Chief, out of the main circle of conversation. I had noticed before that when Jake was forced to appear in public with Donniker, he always tried to fade into the background. After he'd admitted that he had no respect for Donniker and wanted his job, I realized what he was doing. Not surprisingly, he didn't want people to associate him with the Chief.

"You're completely satisfied, then, that Jolene murdered her father and committed suicide?" Cyrus raised the question we'd all been wondering. "Even before the autopsy? There could be no other explanation?"

"We're satisfied," Donniker said smugly.

"But what about the poisonings?" I couldn't resist asking, although we'd all agreed we'd only listen to the Chief and save questions later for Jake. The man was so pompous, though, it was beyond my capabilities for self-control. "Why would anyone want to poison Marie and me?"

"I suggest that you look into your own activities," he said. "Somewhere, amazingly enough, you've irritated someone."

Roberta poked me this time instead of kicking me, but alongside, I heard what sounded like a muted growl emit from Cyrus.

"Oh, come on," I protested. "And Marie?"

He didn't answer.

"Well, I'm not satisfied, Chief," Will said. "I hope you'll keep the case open. I don't believe my sister had it in her to kill herself or anyone else, and I think it's stretching it to think that my mother being poisoned during the same period of time was only a coincidence."

"How did she get there?" Cyrus asked quietly.

"Huh?" Oh, how the Chief's expression reminded me of the one he habitually wore in the sixth grade when he hadn't a clue to what was going on.

"How did Jolene transport herself to this very difficult location?"

"Oh, well," the Chief said, "it develops that she'd visited there many times as a girl. It was a hideout of sorts. She'd know all kinds of ways to get there."

"There aren't 'all kinds of ways,' " Will said. "I tailed my sister there once years ago. She and Mary rowed there in a small boat that belonged to the Larsons. I followed at a distance in our motorboat, just close enough to keep them in sight. There *is* no other way to get there, unless she rappelled down the cliff, and I think that's hardly likely." The mental picture of Jolene dangling from a rope was ludicrous. "Did you find a boat?" he asked insistently.

"No, we didn't find a boat," the Chief said sarcastically. "It's been six weeks. It could have drifted away easily by now."

"Have you had any reports of anyone finding one?" Roberta asked.

"No, but you know as well as I do that if some kids found a rowboat, they might look on it as salvage and not report it."

"How about one that's missing?" Will asked. "Have you checked with the marina to see if she rented one there? And if so, wouldn't they have contacted you when word got around that my sister had disappeared? They couldn't have failed to notice her and perhaps wondered a little what she wanted with a boat, especially if it wasn't returned."

"No, we haven't checked with the marina." The Chief's face was showing hints of the peculiar shade that I'd noticed before. I saw that Jake had removed a small notebook from his breast pocket and was taking notes.

"The body . . ." Cyrus hesitated. "It was evident that it had been there for some time. Have you determined the date of death?" He glanced uneasily at Will.

"Don't worry about upsetting me," Will said. "I can face reality. That's a good question. Did she die at the time she first disappeared, or later?"

"I hope the autopsy will show that," the Chief said, "but there wasn't a great deal . . ." His eyes shifted toward Will. "It doesn't really matter, does it?"

Will appeared to be strong enough to face distasteful matters. That was good. "How did she die? Or wasn't the cause of death obvious?" I asked.

"It was obvious. She shot herself. In the right temple. With the same gun used to kill her father, we feel, although we *are* checking on that, whether you people think we do our job or not. The gun was lying next to the body."

"Hmm," I said as I sensed Will straightening beside me.

"My sister was left-handed," he announced.

"Doesn't mean a thing. Suicides can, and do, choose to use their other hand. Happens all the time. Now, if you people will excuse me, I have a department to run."

"Oh, of course, Chief," I said as sweetly as I could muster. "Do pardon our curiosity."

"Of course." He echoed my words, but his were dripping with condescension.

"Let's go over to the bakery and have something," I suggested, catching Jake's eye. I hoped he'd follow my hint and join us.

"I have one question," I said as soon as we were outside. "Why has the town put up with that inefficient dolt for so many years?"

Cyrus looked at me. "Since you're the only one of us who's been here during his entire tenure, you're the person to answer that question."

That was a stopper. "Umm," I said. "I suppose because of indifference. I never had to deal with him personally before, and it was easier to make jokes about his incompetence than to do something about it. If enough people feel that way, nothing happens."

"When this is over, shall we form a committee?" he asked.

"Absolutely."

"Count me in," Will said.

The bakery wasn't busy this close to noon. The morning coffee people had left and the lunch crowd hadn't started straggling in. We each chose our drinks, and Cyrus brought a plate of fresh doughnuts as we settled in a back corner. "How's your mother managing?" I asked Will.

He shrugged. "The same way she always manages unpleasant news. Controlled. Unemotional. Sometimes I wish she'd scream and pull her hair."

"I don't suppose your father encouraged that sort of behavior," I said.

His mouth twisted. "No. He didn't."

I suspected from the look on his face that Lyle had not only discouraged emotion—and disagreement—but had actively forbidden it. I, for one, think it's much more healthy to rid oneself of negative thoughts. This whole murder situation was beginning more and more to seem as if someone, somewhere, had allowed such thoughts to fester. Perhaps it *was* realistic to assume that Jolene, who'd been so obviously disturbed, had harbored ill will toward her father for many years. Still, I couldn't quite accept that conclusion.

I'd been so absorbed in my contemplation that I hadn't noticed Jake come in the door. Good. Now maybe we'd get some real answers. We pushed chairs around as he went over to the counter for coffee.

"How can you stand to work for that man?" Roberta asked as he sat down and pulled his chair up to the table.

"Can't," Jake said, taking a sip of coffee. "Let's hope we can prove him wrong and get rid of him."

"What can we do?" Will asked. "I don't mean that to sound hopeless, I mean—just give us assignments."

Jake shook his head. "It isn't that simple. I wish it were. Anyway, you've done pretty well on your own, I hate to admit."

"We've stirred things up, anyway," I said.

"Just don't stir too hard. There is one thing the Chief didn't tell you that's interesting," he said.

"What? What?" Cyrus inquired in his usual fashion.

"The gun. The department has had a system for years of putting our mark on any weapon that's used in a crime."

"So?" I inquired, hope rising as I said it. "Are you saying this one is marked?"

He nodded. "Under the grip where we always put it."

"Wonderful. Then you know who owned the gun, at least originally," I said.

"Why do I have the feeling that that was the good news?" Cyrus asked.

Jake grimaced and spread his hands. "Why is it that good news so often has a down side? The bad news is that it doesn't do us a hell of a lot of good. We haven't been using computers as long as most departments. The Chief was more or less forced into it, but he really is from a pre-computer generation. Anyway, this mark indicates that it came through our hands some years ago, before we were putting anything like that in the system."

Years ago, I thought. Just as I'd been surmising. This whole thing was rooted in a past crime, sure as I was sitting here. "But you must have a record somewhere. What good would it do to mark a gun if you didn't record it?" I asked.

"Oh, yeah. We have a record somewhere. In a box in the basement of the police station. Boxes that are filed according to year instead of anything useful."

"Oh, boy," I said, picturing a heap of brown pasteboard cartons with files tumbling out of them. "How can we look at them?"

"You can't. The Chief would never authorize it. Neither would he authorize it on my official time. As far as he's concerned, the case will be closed when the autopsy report comes through."

"Closed and put in a brown box to molder?" Roberta asked.

"No, not that bad. It'll molder on a computer instead."

"Oh, great." I put my hands to my face, mulling over what he'd said.

"You said, 'official time,' Jake." Cyrus as usual, was thinking quickly. "Does that mean you're willing to do some unofficial looking?"

"Absolutely. As I told you . . ." He hesitated, glancing at Will who had, of course, not been in our original discussion. "I'm determined to see a turnaround in this police department. I want to stick with it until it's run as well as any small town can do."

"With you at the helm," Cyrus said. "Just for your information, we at this table are now an *ex-officio* committee to dump Chief Donniker."

Jake grinned. "Good." He stood, draining his cup. "Back to work for me. I'd better clean up some of my official paperwork so I'll have time to poke around down in the dungeon after hours."

Will stood, holding out his hand. "Thanks. I appreciate that."

"You're welcome." Jake shook his hand and started to leave. "That doesn't mean," he said, turning back, "that my previous warnings don't still stand. Come to me with anything you know or even suspect. This murderer has failed twice. I don't expect another failure or that he'll give up."

"Or she," Roberta added.

"Or she. That's a given."

181

CHAPTER XIX

As Jake left, Will glanced at his watch. "I'd better hurry," he said. "I've lost Peter from the store. He took a job with Lowe's Hardware. It's tough finding anyone qualified, and I'm not sure about that new kid I hired."

I'd noticed that he didn't look as if he'd been sleeping well, with dark circles under bloodshot eyes and facial lines etched more deeply than warranted by his years. No wonder. This was a difficult time for him, with just the aspects we were aware of—the deaths of his father and sister, the poisoning of his mother, and now, problems with the store. We knew nothing of his life in Oregon. I hoped, for his sake, that everything there was more serene than on this end. One would think that he'd be eager to return to Portland once everything was resolved.

Except—he'd run away once. Had he gained enough maturity to face problems and resolve them instead? It would appear so, just from the fact that he'd returned, supported his mother and taken over the business.

Or, a niggling voice suggested, did he return because he'd instigated the problems? Could he, in spite of appearances, be the murderer after all? Portland wasn't so far away that he couldn't have zipped up I-5 without anyone knowing. I'd love to find out what was in those papers that Will had referred to in speaking with Roberta. He must have known that there was a possibility his father had left some-

thing that he wouldn't want found by others. His mother?
Or police? And, what was it? Could Roberta possibly worm
it out of Will before she returned, in just such a few days, to
New York?

For an instant, I was on the verge of suggesting he join
Roberta, Cyrus and me the next time we met, but I refrained.
"I hope your new employee works out for you," I said.
"And . . ." I swallowed my reluctance, "let us know when
Jolene's body is released and the funeral scheduled." This fu-
neral was another that I was obligated to attend.

"I'll do that," he promised. Turning to Roberta, he asked,
"Could we meet—maybe for lunch? Tomorrow?"

It would have taken a harder heart than Roberta's to turn
down the plea in his eyes. "I'd like that," she answered.
"Shall I meet you at the store?"

They arranged the time, and then, Will, too, departed.

Cyrus had come to the police department in his car,
saying he had to leave for Seattle afterward. He was
flaunting being secretive about his destination and enjoying every moment. I sniffed as I watched him fold himself into his car. I wasn't going to be so quick to share
theories and hunches with him in the future if he was going
to be like that.

He rolled down the window and spoke. "I hope to pull it
all together and have something to report soon, ladies."

"Maybe." I averted my gaze and deliberately sounded
skeptical.

"Tut-tut, Donna Rose," he said. "Don't get your nose out
of joint. I just want to be sure of my facts before I say anything."

"Of course." I barely glanced as he waved and spun away
from the curb, cutting in front of a green pickup. It would
serve him right if Jake were lurking around the corner and

183

gave him a ticket, but no such luck. Cyrus's driving record, no doubt, had more blemishes on it than just the one we had discussed.

The driver of the pickup was shaking his head as he again accelerated. Beside me, Roberta chuckled. "What an aggravating man. For the first time, I see why he upsets you. Why on earth couldn't he at least give us a hint?"

"That's Cyrus." I grimaced, and then suggested, "Let's go to the P.O." Sometimes it's a nuisance, picking up my mail at the Cedar Harbor Post Office, but the second time the mailbox on the street in front of my house was trashed, I capitulated and began paying for a P.O. box. It still annoys me, though, that the cretins who get their jollies from ruining perfectly good mailboxes and making people's lives difficult should escape without retribution.

The lobby was unusually empty as we unlocked my box. Roberta had a packet forwarded from New York and a letter from Joel, I saw as I pulled out a rather large pile. Her fingers were shaking as she ripped it open. How I wished, yet again, that there was something I could do to make things better for her. She'd been bearing up well, even appearing to be attracted to Will, but I knew her. She'd always tended to keep her emotions to herself, but her hands, and the occasional times I'd noticed her staring into space and being unusually silent, were evidence that the divorce was considerably more traumatic than she admitted.

While she studied the typewritten letter, I busied myself with my own mail. Another postcard from Alice Pierce. She'd worked herself as far south as Zurich. "You'd love it here," she had scribbled in her usual almost indecipherable scrawl. "So neat and prosperous, flowers everywhere, and swans. My toes better now." *Huh* I thought. *Toe?* I'd clearly missed something. Well, the postcard telling about the toe would probably show up later, from Delft or someplace else between Norway and Zurich.

I also had an envelope with the return address stamped in faded ink. CEDAR HARBOR WATER DISTRICT, it said, and gave the box number used by the board. Probably the notice of the annual meeting, I thought, laying it aside and shuffling through the rest of the pile. A Lands' End catalog and one from Eddie Bauer. How I love both stores and how I wished they each didn't send so many catalogs. I used to enjoy them so much more when they came only seasonally.

Beside me, I heard Roberta sigh and the rustle of paper as she stuffed the letter back in its envelope. I waited for a comment but none was forthcoming. Finally, looking sheepish, she said, "It was just a note enclosing a copy of some papers from Joel's attorney. Did you get anything interesting?"

"A card from Alice. Sometimes I wish I'd gone with her. Just think, I'd have missed all this."

She glanced at me sideways with a small smile. Could she be thinking that I wouldn't want to miss the summer's activities in Cedar Harbor? Life was so pleasant before Cyrus, before the water board, before murder. *Before it became interesting?* That infuriating small voice inside my head whispered until I squelched it.

We'd arrived home, eaten lunch and were lingering over our drinks when I returned to the stack of mail and ripped open the missive from the water board. I was right. It was a notice of the annual meeting, which was scheduled for the hall at the Lutheran Church. It was always assumed that so many people would be thrilled to come that they didn't dare hold it at the library, but this seldom occurred. As long as water flows, people aren't interested unless their rates are going to go up.

I turned to the second page, which contained the agenda I

had prepared. The subjects to be discussed were all routine: a report from Kirk Bentner, our maintenance manager, a discussion of upgrading the pipes in the Highland section of town, which consistently had low pressure. There was no mention of Shadybrook Meadows or any other controversial subject.

The last item was the election of new board members. There were two vacancies to be filled: a replacement for Lyle and the regular spot, which was opening because Michael had completed his three years and was not interested in re-election. I didn't have to wonder why.

The election of new board members was likely to be uncontested. Only rarely has anyone been nominated from the floor. Basically, being on the board is not one of the more desired plums of local politics. It involves unpaid hassle, and no one in his right mind ever accepts a second term. "Right mind," of course doesn't include power-hungry males such as Lyle had been, and of course Al. Lyle had been a fixture on the board as long as I could remember. So, each year, someone new was coerced into running.

This year, no surprises, but I'd completely put the subject out of my mind. The new nominees were Susan Reilly and Will Corrigan. I realized that I'd never discussed the water board with Will. He'd indicated that he hadn't made up his mind about staying in town, and yet here he was, running for the board.

And Sue. I knew about her, of course, but seeing it in print reminded me that Sue had been evasive when I'd questioned her earlier. Why had I let her get away with it?

Of course, if I was right about long-ago events being at the root of our current evil, then Sue, Mark, Al and Shadybrook Meadows had nothing to do with it. Still, I couldn't be sure, and I'd taken this on as my share of our investigating. Cyrus was irritating, but I do not renege on a duty I've promised to fulfill.

I reached for the telephone. "I'm going to call Sue," I said to Roberta, who was engrossed again in studying the papers from Joel. She nodded and didn't answer as I punched in the number.

"Sue," I said, after she'd answered and we'd exchanged greetings, "you never did stop by and meet my daughter, and she's only going to be here a few more days."

"I know," she said, sounding guilty. "I've been so busy. And so have you. Finding bodies, among other things."

"Well, that really took only half a day. This time, maybe a little longer than that, what with the police and all. Jake is such a treasure, though, and so helpful." I introduced his name on purpose to see what reaction I elicited, but it didn't work.

"Umm," she said. "I could stop by this afternoon, if you're going to be home. It's a nice day and I'd enjoy a walk with the boys."

"Sounds good. We can sit outside if it isn't too hot. I've moved the table and chairs over into the shade, though, and it's usually quite pleasant. What time?"

"Three o'clock?"

"Dandy. See you then." I hung up, and spoke to Roberta. "I committed you, too."

"So I noticed." But she smiled as she said it. I'd been reasonably sure that she had no plans, since she wasn't seeing Will again until tomorrow.

Susan arrived with Todd and Jeff a little after three, and I was pleased when she and Roberta hit it off immediately. Roberta was entranced with the boys. She had been unable to have children but always liked them, another reason that I felt she would have been—or could be—a good teacher.

I always was glad to have the opportunity to take advantage of my, if I do say so myself, unusually beautiful garden. It wasn't quite as pretty now, in August, as it had been earlier, but still, it would have been difficult to find another so fine in Cedar Harbor. I'm especially fond of the chrysanthemums of fall, which were beginning their show, but the hollyhocks, asters and daylilies were in fine fettle. Sue was suitably appreciative, especially when I offered to give her starts after I divided perennials.

"I'd love that," she said. "I've often wished—but I didn't want to ask."

"You should have," Roberta assured her. "There's nothing Mom likes better."

Somehow the subject of the water board hadn't come up. When the conversation even headed in that direction, Sue diverted it. At first I thought it was an accident, but then I decided she was doing it deliberately. I was going to have to be blunt.

"Sue," I began, "I've been meaning to ask you more about the water board situation."

"Oh?" She raised an eyebrow. "What situation?"

"Well, the election is coming up, and I think we all need to know where everyone stands on issues. What do you think of Shadybrook Meadows?"

"I really haven't an opinion yet. Have you made up your mind?"

"Well, actually, not totally."

"Good. Mark says . . ."

She stopped speaking in the middle of her sentence. The way her lips jammed together made it evident she *had* been avoiding the subject. However, she'd said it and it gave me the opportunity I needed.

"Mark . . ." I mused. "You seem to have become good friends with him."

She shrugged. "Why not?"

"Well, Jake . . ."

"Jake has shown no interest in me. I gave him every signal I could think of and he didn't follow up. What other choice did I have?"

"Hit him over the head." That idiot. So he was the one to blow it.

"Mother," Roberta said, laughing. "We don't quite do it that way these days."

Sue smiled at her. "Right. So . . . Mark *is* interested. What was I to do?"

I could think of several things, but that wasn't the issue right now. "But Mark . . . Shadybrook Meadows . . ."

Her eyes narrowed. "Just what are you inferring?"

"I'm not inferring. I'm asking. Did Mark have anything to do with you changing your mind about being on the board?"

Now she stood. "I don't really see what business it is of yours."

"Because I care about Cedar Harbor." I wasn't going to back down this time. Roberta swung her gaze between us, her expression worried.

"Yes," Sue said defiantly. "I am able to be on the board because Mark very generously made it possible. His little sister is going to babysit for me. I didn't ask if he was going to pay her. But Mark has never once tried to influence me in any way about Shadybrook Meadows, and he's too fine a person to do so. Donna, we've been friends a long time, but I resent the implication.

"Come on, boys," she said, unfolding the stroller, "we're going home."

I was silent. I'd found out what I wanted to know. But what good did it do? Perhaps Mark really was interested in Sue as a person, not a vote. He was the only one who knew,

189

and he wasn't about to talk to me. As to whether Shadybrook
Meadows, his complicity in getting Sue on the board, or anything about that situation was connected with the murder, I
was no closer to finding out.

All I'd done was ruin a perfectly good friendship.

CHAPTER XX

I felt down all day. I'd become very fond of Sue. Roberta was leaving in just a few days, which was depressing enough. My friendship with Sue had brought youth into my life and helped alleviate the loneliness caused by Roberta's absence. And what had I gained from my questioning? Nothing, that's what. Well, maybe I could make up for it by putting a bug in Jake's ear. Perhaps in time she would forgive me.

I heard the roar of Cyrus returning as I watered in late afternoon. You'd think they'd require better mufflers on cars such as his. I yanked the hose hard, almost uprooting the long-suffering Russell lupine, which had been recovering from its earlier difficulty.

We had a light supper, and at nine-thirty I told Roberta I was going to retire early. I hoped a good night's sleep would restore my equanimity.

"Good night," she answered. "Sleep tight. And don't worry. You did what you had to. What you said was harsh, maybe, but when this is over, she'll forgive you."

"I hope so," I said dourly, heading for my room.

In the morning, I did feel better. For a while. I completed my watering early, then cleaned the kitchen, tackling the rings on the stove and the mess under the sink. There is nothing that makes one feel more virtuous than completing those two jobs.

I felt good, until just a few minutes after Roberta left to walk to town to meet Will for lunch. The phone rang, and I innocently went to answer it.

"Mrs. Galbreath?" a faintly familiar voice said. "This is Kirk Bentner."

"Well, hi, Kirk. What can I do for you?" Again innocently, I assumed he'd called about water district business.

In a way he had. "Well, uh," he began, noticeably stumbling over his words, "I've been meaning to call. We've had several complaints . . ."

If people would just learn to come to the point and be concise, I thought. I always tried to instill this in my pupils, but Kirk had attended school elsewhere. Whatever the problem was, it must be serious for him to contact board members individually instead of waiting for a meeting. "Complaints? How can I help you?" I asked.

"Well, it seems . . . well, it seems that people think you haven't been following the rules for watering. And that as a member of the board, you . . ."

"Cyrus!" I exploded. "Cyrus complained."

"Uh, well actually . . ."

"Never mind. I'll take care of it. Thank you for calling." I slammed the receiver down.

The rat! He'd always said he was going to report me but I never truly believed that he would. Especially after we'd declared a truce, way back when we began to work together. I'd felt that we'd almost—not quite, but almost—become friends. We'd never be intimates, I was sure of that, no matter what we shared. But now . . . enemies!

I threw open the front door and charged across the grass to Cyrus's porch. I pounded on the door.

"Donna Rose!" Cyrus peered through the opened doorway. "Whatever is the matter?"

"Matter? Matter? You betrayed me. You're a weasel, a . . ." I paused, trying to think of another unpleasant animal.

He glanced around quickly before he said, "You'd better come in."

Over my shoulder, I could see the Moores standing near their car and staring in fascination. Oh, great. Now everyone in Cedar Harbor would hear about our set-to. "I suppose so." I stepped over the threshold.

"I haven't the slightest idea what you're talking about." He shut the door behind me. "Now, calm down and tell me what's the matter. To my knowledge, I haven't done anything . . ."

"Haven't done anything? You reported me to the water board. I mean, I'm *on* the water board and we didn't discuss it. You reported me to Kirk Bentner for watering on the wrong day. He said several times."

"Now, wait a minute. Once. A long time ago, that first time I threatened to. Did it ever occur to you that others might notice your disregard for the rules? People who do what they're supposed to resent those who don't—like you, Donna Rose." He waggled a finger in front of my nose.

"I don't believe you. Nobody else would be mean enough."

"Oops," he said, turning suddenly. "I'd better turn off my iron. Then we can continue this fascinating discussion." He hurried down the hall. I followed.

Like me, he used his third bedroom for a workspace and for storage. I iron in mine, too. The resemblance ended there. Whereas mine has projects in process scattered around, a sewing machine set up on an old desk, mending piled nearby, his was neat. Labeled boxes, boxes that all matched in color and dimension, were arranged on shelves. He had one of those doohickeys for hanging freshly ironed shirts conveniently at hand, with several crisp, freshly laundered ones in evidence. And—he had stacks of tee shirts and undergarments. All ironed, all folded perfectly square, without a smidgen sticking out of place. On the board was a pair of red paisley shorts.

"Cyrus," I said, "surely you don't iron your underwear?"

He stiffened. Everything grew stiff. His back, his arms, his moustache. His cold eyes, boring into mine. "Of course."

"Don't you know you'll ruin the elastic?"

He took me by the arm as his left hand yanked the cord from the socket.

"You shouldn't treat electrical cords like that either," I informed him.

He steered me out of the room and shut the door behind us. "You are an exasperating woman, Donna Rose."

"Likewise. Why did you make all those complaints about me?"

"I did not make *all those complaints*. I made one complaint. I made it before I found out what a *charming*, interesting woman you really were behind that facade of eccentricity."

"Me?"

"You."

For a moment we stood there, staring at each other. The sound of someone breathing hard reverberated in the hall. Finally, I said, "I should never have trusted a man who irons his underwear."

"Perhaps I shouldn't trust a woman who doesn't."

Even in the darkness of the hall, I caught the glint in his eyes that just might mean he was laughing at me. I turned and fled.

Roberta arrived home in the middle of the afternoon. I'd been holding in my frustration all afternoon, waiting for her to arrive so I could complain. "Can you believe it?" I asked. "That miserable man reported me to Kirk Bentner."

"Who's Kirk?" she asked.

"Oh, I forgot, you wouldn't know him. He runs the water district for us. Very capable. Or, at least I've always thought so until now. But Cyrus . . ." I suddenly had second thoughts about telling Roberta the whole story. I remembered her reaction to the slug episode.

"Cyrus what?" I didn't answer. "Mom," she said, "you might as well tell me. Have you two been at it again?"

So I told her. I've never been very good at prevaricating. "And, would you believe it? He was ironing his underwear and folding it into neat stacks, and . . ."

"I don't think ironing and folding neatly is classified as a sin." She studied me, her head cocked to one side.

Inwardly, I began to cringe. Now that I had told, I wasn't so sure of my ground. It was not a scene that I would have cared to have anyone witness. "I still feel I'm right about the watering. I have no choice. There is no way to maintain my garden on that unreasonable schedule."

"Why don't you get them to change it? I've heard you grumble about it ever since they put the restrictions on, before you were on the board."

"I tried once, but no one on the board cared."

"And you didn't try again?"

"Well, I haven't exactly been on the best of terms with the others . . ."

She shook her head at me and then sighed.

"I guess that's the end of our working with Cyrus."

"Oh, no, you don't." Now *she* waggled a finger at me. "He's been a big help. He saved our lives, remember that. Besides, I have something to report."

"What?" I realized, then, that she'd had a very satisfied, almost smug expression plastered on her face when she came in the door. If I hadn't been so engrossed in my own problems, it would have registered.

"I think I'll wait. I . . ." she stood and headed for the phone, "am going to call Cyrus and invite him over right now for a meeting. Maybe I can offer *quid pro quo* and we can find out what he's been up to. What's his number?"

Cyrus had a large sack in his arms when Roberta let him in the door. "Here," he said, walking over and handing it to me. "It's a special variety of very sweet white corn that ripens earlier than most. Thought you could use it for your dinner."

"How nice," Roberta said, as I took it. "I love corn, and I thought I'd miss the season here. I never get it really fresh in New York."

"In that case," he said, making a mock bow, "I shall see that you are supplied with all you can eat until you leave." He glanced back at me, waiting, expression unreadable.

"Thank you," I forced out, not quite meeting his eyes. Truth to tell, I was afraid that if I did, I would burst out laughing. It had been a shameful scene, as Roberta had gently pointed out after she'd talked to Cyrus and arranged for him to come over. I wasn't sure what it was about the man that made me do these things. I hoped that none of my former students would hear about either slugs or underwear. I certainly wouldn't tell anyone, although I wasn't sure about Cyrus.

"I'll put it in the refrigerator," Roberta offered, taking the sack from me. "Then we can talk." Her voice was faintly muffled as she bent over and shuffled things to make room. "Let's go outside. I've got the lemonade." She emerged, holding the pitcher.

"Roberta," I said, taking the pitcher from her, "you are going to drive me insane if you stall. I want to hear what you found out, I'd like to hear what Cyrus is chasing down, and I wish everyone would quit playing games."

Roberta and Cyrus glanced at each other, and a look of understanding passed between them. I turned my back and reached for the tray and added glasses.

"I guess the strain is getting to all of us," I said. "I'm sorry, Cyrus." I stared at the counter. "I should have inquired about Kirk's call in a thoughtful manner. Did you really report me only once, a long time ago?"

"Cross my heart."

"Then I wonder who . . . ?"

"Don't worry 'who,' Mom. Just get the board to come up with more rational hours. I'll bet Cyrus would back you."

"Within reason," he said. "And I'm sorry, too."

That was as much as I could expect from him. Neither of us said anything about underwear, and I doubted if either of us would, ever again.

"I'll start it off," Roberta said as soon as we were settled outside in the shade. A leaf drifted down. My dogwood. They anticipate fall before any of the other deciduous trees are thinking about shedding.

"Will is in the clear. His company had sent him to San Francisco on business at the time his father was killed. They had to track him down and arrange for a substitute so that he could come home for the funeral."

"Good," I said. "I like him and I'm relieved, although I had come to the conclusion that he was much too nice to be a murderer."

"Nice doesn't stop people sometimes," Cyrus said dolefully.

"Maybe not, but I'm still glad."

"Incidentally, I found out why Lyle was so adamantly opposed to Shadybrook Meadows," Roberta continued.

"Oh?" Cyrus said. "I had wondered. It seemed strange, especially when his best friend, Al, is so strongly in favor of the development."

"Marie told Will that Lyle got into an argument with Mark at a poker game. It escalated, one of those silly, childish things, and Mark took his business elsewhere. His considerable business. Lyle never forgave him."

"Is that all you have to report, Roberta?" I asked.

"No, it isn't. Will told me what he was hunting for in his father's papers and what he found." She grinned. "Interested?"

That made Cyrus straighten in his chair. "What? What?"

"Your turn," she said leaning back. "I'll tell you when you tell us what you've been finding out. It isn't really fair, you know, to keep secrets."

"Oh, very well. I was almost ready . . ." He took a sip of lemonade and cleared his throat.

To start the ball rolling, I asked, "Have you found out whether Lyle did anything underhanded to get the county to slap on a moratorium?"

"He at the very least wined and dined county officials. Whether I can prove more than that, I don't know. I'll take what I have to the authorities when it's appropriate, but whether they'll want to follow up now that Lyle's dead . . ." He shrugged. "As for the rest, there were things about Shadybrook Meadows that intrigued me. The company isn't owned entirely by Mark Gasper, you know."

"Oh? Those big ones usually aren't owned by just one person, are they?" I asked.

198

"No, but have you ever heard anything about other investors in this one?"

I shook my head.

"There are actually several. But the largest, aside from Mark, is . . . get this, Al Parry."

"No kidding!" I set my glass down. "The old phony. We can get him off the water board. I don't think it helps us with the murder, but . . ."

"Why? He's obviously been hiding his connection with Shadybrook Meadows."

"Admittedly, but I can't see him murdering to prevent people finding out. It is a matter of public record, after all."

"But what," Roberta suggested slowly, "if Mark had to let Al into the deal because Al's blackmailing him or something?"

"My thoughts exactly," Cyrus said. "That's what I'm trying to find out."

"Any leads?" I asked.

"Not great ones, I must admit."

"Well, I still think the murders are rooted in the past. I have a feeling . . ."

"Your hunches have been good, I must admit," Cyrus said, "but I think you're stretching this time. What evidence do you have?"

"The gun. Where has it been all these years? I do wish Jake would find the proper file and get back to us."

"I'll concede that the murder is related to something in the past, but what if that past event was something Mark did, and Al was blackmailing him?"

I sighed. "That's as good as any premise, I guess. But what are we going to do about Al? Call someone on the City Council?"

"I had something in mind, if you agree. How about

waiting for the water district meeting and springing it there? In front of everyone?"

"What a terrific idea," Roberta said. "And I won't be here! What a bummer. I want to see it."

"Your mother," Cyrus said, preening his moustache, "will be delighted to give you a blow-by-blow, I'm sure."

"Absolutely. For once, I'm looking forward to that darn meeting."

CHAPTER XXI

"Now, my closemouthed daughter, I am as anxious as Cyrus, no doubt, to hear what Will had to say about those papers."

"It seems," Roberta rubbed her nose and smiled, "that old Lyle, the stalwart of the community, had a collection of pornography."

"Oh-ho! I see." Her news presented a new dimension of the man, but it was going to take some getting used to. Lyle had even run for the school board some years previously, and he was always there lending a hand at local functions, albeit a hand that wanted to be at the upper level of management. Stalwarts of the community could be hiding vile acts as well as anyone else, and I should have known so.

"How did Will find out?" Cyrus asked.

"He'd seen some of it, back before he ran away from home. In fact, that's when they had their last argument, the one that made him leave. The old jerk was mad because Will had been in his study. Never mind that he was looking for some carbon paper for a report he was doing for school."

"Sounds a little weak to me," Cyrus said. "Lyle probably would have kept his porn collection under lock and key, particularly if he was hiding it from his wife and children, which I assume he would."

Roberta agreed. "That thought occurred to me. But, since Will was in the process of sharing a deeply-felt secret, and it took some doing to get him to that point, I didn't want to interrupt or to appear that I was pumping him for information. Anyway, Lyle accused him of snooping—as I suspect he was—slugged him one time too many, and Will left."

"I wonder if Marie knows." I was picturing her face as she described why she, alone, had to go through those papers.

"Will thought not. At least, protecting his mother from finding the stuff was the reason he gave for searching behind her back. I assume he's checked the family computer, too, but I didn't ask him."

"I don't suppose he'd have wanted anyone else to find out, either, even though he didn't get along with his father," Cyrus interjected. "Family members so often have a mix of hate-love, but get protective when their own pride is at stake. An evil-doing of one reflects on the others, that sort of thinking."

Cyrus chewed on his lower lip for a moment, then asked, "What are we going to do about it?"

Roberta was horrified. "Nothing! I promised Will. Sleazy secrets aren't that uncommon. I could see, maybe, someone murdering to keep his secret. But why would anyone murder Lyle because he got his jollies from pictures of obscene acts?"

"His family?" I said reluctantly. "And, especially, Marie, since we seem to have eliminated Will as a possibility?"

"Then why was she poisoned?" Roberta asked.

"Well, then we're back to the possibility that she faked it, then tried to poison me to take away any suspicion from herself."

"Oh, God," Roberta said. "And I promised him."

"You're forgetting one other possibility," Cyrus said.

We both turned and looked at him. I, with dismay, got where he was driving first. "Jolene."

He nodded. "Jolene. She could have found out her father's secret. So, she decided to kill him."

"All these years later?" Roberta asked. "Why wait?"

"Because it took that long to fester. Because she didn't have the opportunity before. *I* don't know why. I never understood why anyone considered murder as an option in the first place," he said.

Not for the first time, I wondered about the conflict between Cyrus's principles and the career he had chosen. "But where did she get the gun? The one that Jake says was involved in a previous crime in Cedar Harbor?"

Glumly, we stared at each other. Then Roberta said, "I can't help it. I promised Will. All I can do is try to persuade him that he should go to the police with this himself. I sure look forward to suggesting that his mother or his sister killed his father."

"And you have only two days to convince him," I reminded her. "Two days and it's back to New York."

"Well, can I sleep on it?" she asked, her face haggard. "I really like Will, just as a friend, of course."

"Certainly," Cyrus said. "Perhaps there's another way. Surely he knows you were going to tell us?"

She nodded.

"Well, then, perhaps one of us should approach him."

Oh, boy, I thought. Just what I wanted to do. I'd already done so much blundering, with Marie and now Sue. All I wanted to do was hurt someone else, especially if it turned out to be unnecessary. "I agree with Roberta," I said. "Let's all sleep on it. Maybe we'll come up with an alternative."

Before we had a chance to get together, I had a phone call from Jake. Roberta and I were just finishing breakfast after a sleepless night for each of us.

"Have some news," Jake said after identifying himself.

"Oh? Something useful, I hope."

"Should be. I've found the right old file and I know when the gun was used."

"Wonderful. Roberta, Jake found information about the gun," I said in an aside, and her face lit up. "Thank you, Jake, for looking. We appreciate it."

"I'm doing it for myself, too, remember," he said.

"But, who? What crime?" I asked impatiently.

"Well, now, I'm going to have to ask you to be patient for a bit. Just a little, I hope. I need to ask some questions, but I promise to get back to you as soon as I can."

"Today?" I urged.

"I hope so. If she . . ."

He stopped speaking, then went on while my mind was whirling through all the potential "shes" that were connected to the case. Marie leapt to mind first and foremost.

"I didn't mean even to say that much. If I can reach the woman in question today, I'll call and come over. You guys deserve that much," he said.

"Good luck. I hope . . . I hope this is the end."

"So do we all, Donna. I'll get back to you." And he hung up.

Needless to say, we were in a turmoil all day. At least Roberta and I were. Cyrus, when I called him, said, "Well, in that case, I'll run in and get my oil changed. Doesn't sound as if you'll hear from him that soon."

"No, I don't suppose so," I admitted, "but I can't stand to leave the phone."

"I'm sure you've heard the old adage about watched pots . . ."

"Never, Cyrus," I said sarcastically. Seemed like I used that tone with him a lot. "You must think that I've lived in an isolation bubble all my life. But pots or not, I couldn't possibly force myself to go away from this house until we hear from Jake."

"To each his own. Call me when you hear."

I cleaned the bathrooms this time. All that nervous energy had to be put to some use. Roberta did laundry, confirmed her airline ticket and organized her things for the trip home. Along the way, we discussed Will.

I didn't have to broach the subject, since we were discussing how we were going to handle the touchiness of persuading him he should tell Jake about the pornography. It was increasingly evident that the duty would fall on me. A woman, we agreed, would more likely have the subtle manner necessary to convince him. "I could do it," Roberta offered, but it was evident she was very reluctant. I would be the heavy, I told her firmly.

"You seem to be fond of Will," I commented.

"I am. I feel sorry for him. He's a nice guy trapped in a horrible situation."

"I meant as maybe a bit more than a friend?" I waited anxiously for her reaction.

"Maybe," she admitted. "But he's here and I'm going to be there, and besides, I'm certainly not ready for a relationship."

"Just keep in mind what a dysfunctional family he comes from." I know the experts say one should not give advice to children, particularly one as mature as Roberta. But how can a mother resist? Isn't that what we're here for? Roberta's used to me and has never appeared to object to my counseling.

"I think he avoided the worst of it by leaving. He seems stable. As you always say, he 'has his head screwed on right.' Besides, almost everyone I know comes from a dysfunctional family, by present definitions. Even us." She folded a skirt and laid it in her suitcase.

"Us?"

"Well, certainly. A single parent household with no father. Not your fault, of course, and . . ." She looked up and caught the expression on my face. "I think I'm even stronger than most because of it, because you did such a terrific job and set such a good example."

"Well, I tried."

How was I going to bear having Roberta so far away again after this interlude? I decided I'd said enough about Will. She *was* capable of making sensible decisions, and I should have known that.

In the afternoon, shortly after I heard the roar of Cyrus's returning vehicle, I gave up and went outside to work. I'd really been neglecting things these past weeks, what with one thing and another. Thus it was Roberta who took Jake's call. She stuck her head out the back door and called, "Jake's coming over. He wouldn't tell me anything on the phone. I'll call Cyrus."

"I heard you," boomed his voice across the fence. "I'll be right there."

Roberta and I looked at each other and we both laughed. I leaned my rake against the house and went in. Cyrus arrived shortly after, again with gifts from the garden. "A special lettuce," he said, "that bears the heat quite well. Of course, our heat is nothing compared to the Midwest. And more corn. These tomatoes are nice, if I say so myself. Earlier this year than last because of the warm, dry summer. Peas didn't like it, though," he grumbled as he laid his produce out on the counter.

"That's very nice of you," I said. "Here, let me put them in the refrigerator." I didn't tell him that I'd just yesterday bought some lovely beefsteak tomatoes from Yakima, but that was all right. I love them when they're in season, and they'd get eaten.

We all lifted our heads when we heard the car draw up in front. Roberta let Jake in.

He removed his hat and wiped his forehead, making his red hair stand on end. "Well, I talked to her, but I'm afraid it doesn't help much."

"Who?" we all chorused. Jake, too, should have had lessons in coming to the point.

"Gloria Larson. The gun belonged to her husband, he brought it back from the Korean War."

He took a deep breath, and then he told us. "It's the gun that Mary Larson used to kill herself."

CHAPTER XXII

"Oh, my God!" His words pierced my soul. The gun that killed poor Mary all those years ago. And Jolene . . . "Where has it been all that time?" I asked. "Jolene couldn't possibly have gotten her hands on it back when she was twelve. How did anyone get it from the police after someone was shot with it?"

"Why anyone would want it back is more to the point," Jake said. "Particularly the father of the girl who died. But, according to Gloria, her husband wanted it because he'd had it ever since he picked it up in Korea during the war. An old Smith & Wesson '38 revolver."

"Sit down, Jake," I suggested, "and tell us all the details." We all sat, but I was hardly aware of doing so myself, and I don't think anyone else was either. Otherwise, Cyrus would have never chosen the old rocker that had belonged to my grandmother.

"How could he stand to look at it ever again?" Roberta asked, aghast.

"And the police let it go?" I was amazed.

"When the gun wasn't used for a murder and the family wants it, yes. According to Gloria, it was a symbol to her husband. He used to drink too much, hold it in his hands and weep. She was never sure whether he was weeping for Mary or for dead comrades. She always left the room when he got like that. Anyway, when he died, she looked for the gun with every intent of getting rid of it, but couldn't find it. She assumed he'd thrown it away, but it's entirely possible that he sold the gun. To someone here in Cedar Harbor, obviously."

"Hard to believe." Cyrus sounded stern. "No one would sell a gun that was a symbol, to him, of tragedy. Bury it, maybe."

"How about giving it away?" Roberta suggested.

Jake shrugged. "I'm afraid we'll never know. It could have been stolen. Mr. Larson has been dead for fifteen years, so the gun's been missing for a long time. It could have changed hands since, several times even, and the owner may have never known that it was used by Mary."

"I don't believe it. Too much coincidence. Jolene had to have known what gun . . . I mean . . ."

Jake finished my sentence for me. "You mean, if she killed herself, like the Chief thinks."

"Well, yes. I suppose so. But that still doesn't feel right to me. Well, of course it doesn't. I think we all agreed that the missing boat, combined with the fact the wound was on the wrong side of the head, eliminates that. How very confusing."

"I agree. How confusing." Jake stood, replacing his hat squarely on his head. "I'd hoped to bring better news. As it is, we're no closer to a solution. Which brings up another point. We still have a murderer out there, one who tried to poison you, Donna. I hope you haven't let that out of your mind for one instant, even though there's been no attempt for a while. Are you being careful?"

"Being careful? How can I? Of course I won't taste any anonymous cookies. Do you think whoever it is used poison because he or she didn't have the gun available anymore?"

"That's a possibility. But it really isn't that difficult to buy another. I wouldn't take anything for granted. I wish we knew," he said, narrowing his eyes, "why you're a threat."

"Isn't it obvious?" Cyrus said. "She's been butting in, asking questions."

"So have you all. My warning extends to the three of you. If somehow you are getting close, any of you may be in danger."

"What if," I mused, "the attempt on me wasn't because of my questions but because of something *I* did in the past . . . or didn't do? The connection seems to be coming closer. Mary . . . Jolene."

"But what did you ever have to do with Lyle?" Roberta asked. "Oh, of course. The water board."

"If the connection was the water board, there would have to be something that Lyle and I agreed on for someone to want to murder both of us. We never agreed. Except possibly on Shadybrook Meadows. Anyway, what could the water board have to do with Jolene?"

"I have to go," Jake said, "but keep my warning in mind."

"I will. I promise. And, thanks." I accompanied him to the door, opening it for him. "Oh, Jake," I said as he started down the front walk, "just a minute. I wanted to talk to you."

I shot a meaningful glance at Roberta. She'd know what I had in mind. She frowned and I wondered why, but I pulled the door shut behind me.

"Jake," I said, catching up with him, "I spoke with Sue Reilly the other day."

"Oh?" His tone was of complete lack of interest.

"I'm afraid I distressed her by asking questions. I know I did. But I felt I had to find out. I asked her about changing her mind and joining the water board. I was right. Mark Gasper had everything to do with it. She insisted he was making no attempt to influence her, but he arranged for his little sister to babysit so that Sue was free to go."

"Her arrangements are entirely her own business. I told you that the other day." He opened the door of his patrol car and leaned on it.

"But they should be yours, too! Jake, don't be a dunce. Sue gave every indication of being interested in you; she *wants* you to call her."

"Sure." He straightened. "Did anyone ever tell you you're a busybody? That's what my mother would have called it." He softened his words with a tiny smile.

"Frequently."

"You're imagining things, Donna," he said gently. "Reading things into her words that she didn't mean."

"I'm not. I didn't have to. She flat out-and-out told me. Ask Roberta. She was there; she heard her, too. If you sit around and let a nice girl like her get away, Jake, it's your own fault."

"A nice girl that lets a sleaze like Mark Gasper manipulate her?"

"That's not fair. You've never been in the shoes of a single mother trying to make ends meet. I have. I understand." Well, sort of. I might not have accepted Mark's offer had I been in her position, but I did know that I would have at least considered it.

"Does this mean that you're accepting her word that he hasn't attempted to place her there as an insider?"

I thought for a second before I answered, not having analyzed my reaction before. "Yes. I accept it. I've known Sue for some time and I should have realized. I'm just sorry that I've upset her and I hope she'll forgive me."

He nodded, his face impassive. "Thank you." Then he slid into his car and, with a wave, was gone.

Would he take action? I wasn't sure, but I'd done what I could. I returned to the house.

211

"Mother," Roberta said as I walked in the door, "you didn't actually tell Jake what Sue said, did you?"

"Well, of course not. I mean, not the actual words."

She sighed. "I don't believe it. I didn't think you actually meant to butt in."

"I told you I was going to speak to Jake, and you didn't object then."

"That was because, number one, you were very upset at the moment and, number two, I didn't believe you."

Cyrus sat there grinning and listening. I turned my back on him. "It was my duty," I told her. "Do you really think I shouldn't have interfered?"

Roberta suddenly chuckled. "What's done is done, Mom, don't look so distressed. No, I don't think you should interfere in other people's lives, but I've got to admit that Jake evidently needed some prodding. Maybe it'll work out for the best."

Cyrus leaned back and began to hum. It took me a moment to recognize the tune. "Matchmaker, Matchmaker," that lovely song from *Fiddler on the Roof*. I stuck out my tongue.

The next two days passed in a whirlwind. Jolene's body was released much more quickly than I would have expected, and the funeral had been scheduled for the day after we spoke with Jake. I planned to go, and Roberta felt that she, too, should attend because of her friendship with Will. Cyrus insisted that he would accompany us.

We agreed that we'd delay speaking to Will about his father's hobby. A few days more now wouldn't matter, and it did seem callous to introduce the question of his family's involvement in the murders at this time of mourning.

The funeral was just a funeral, albeit a well-attended one. People who had scarcely known Jolene, if at all, stood around with mock faces of tragedy. That is, some did. Others wore expressions of avid curiosity. I could not see what good the affair did for anyone. Jolene certainly couldn't benefit. Marie was pale and vastly older looking as she leaned on Will's arm. He didn't look too hot himself. I know there are those who feel such occasions are a letting go, the beginning of a period of healing. In this family, the letting go had occurred years before. The only reason to have one now was for appearance's sake, and in my opinion, that is rarely a valid reason for doing anything.

I did, fortuitously, accomplish one thing. At the gathering afterwards, I saw Carrie across the room, cup of tea in hand, as she spoke with the minister. I was surprised that she had come, considering her attitude towards Lyle, but then I realized that she would feel obligated to attend as President of the Historical Society, since Jolene had become a member. Carrie would not let personal feelings intrude.

A sudden thought occurred to me. Carrie had been a businesswoman. She liked staying busy. She needed money. Might not she be just the person Will needed at the hardware store? I knew, through the years, that she'd learned a great deal about some of the products carried there as, like me, she'd been forced to learn. Home repairs, not to mention improvements, are expensive unless one does them herself, and most single women must.

To work for Will, she'd have to forget her earlier disagreements with Lyle. The enlarged hardware store was a fact. She wasn't going to change that. I'd need to convince her that Will was nothing like his father, that he'd be a good man to work for. She'd been her own boss, too, and working for someone else would be different. Still, it seemed an idea worth exploring. Her being employed would solve problems for both of them.

★ ★ ★ ★ ★

I saw that Will, for the first time, was standing alone, his eyes distant, the coffee in his hand untouched. I approached him, offering my condolences.

He took my hand. "If it hadn't been for you," he said, "we might never have found her. I won't forget that. Bad as it is, I already see signs that Mom's improving. Knowing is best."

I agreed, and we exchanged a few more platitudes regarding death. Then I broached the subject of Carrie. "Did you ever know Carrie Sanderson?" I asked. "Used to have the gift shop next door to the hardware store? She's standing over there, speaking to the minister."

He glanced in that direction, then shook his head. "I don't believe so. Well, maybe. Does her husband work at the bank?"

"Did," I answered. "Before he died a few years back." I proceeded to tell him Carrie's history, including her interpretation of Lyle's undercutting her store.

"It occurred to me that she might be the answer to your problem of finding a good employee," I said, "if you have no objection to a woman. She's well liked, intelligent, knows how to keep books . . ."

"Of course I don't mind a woman," he answered. "How about you? Would you like a job?"

I was pleased to see tense lines in his face relax. Taking his attention away from the disagreeable occasion had been a good idea. I shook my head, though. "Thanks. I appreciate your confidence. But do think about Carrie."

"I will," he said. "Do you think she'll want to have anything to do with the store after my father shafted her?"

"I think so. Give me a couple of days to talk to her," I suggested.

Across the room near the door, I could see Cyrus and

Roberta, obviously eager to leave, so I was relieved when the next mourner came up and pressed Will's hand and I could slip unobtrusively away.

The next day was a sad one for me, when Roberta had to leave. I wanted to go to the airport with her but she told me that was silly, given the fact that she had to return the rental car. "You always say you detest the airport run," she reminded me.

I capitulated. Watching a dear one depart on a plane that may or may not have been maintained in tip-top fashion, after standing around a crowded concourse for much too long, had never been high on my want-to-do list, and it was even worse now with the security that prevented anyone but the passenger from passing through.

So, we said goodbye standing in my driveway. We hugged and Roberta wiped away a tear. "Call me," she said. "Keep me informed. Be careful, Mom."

"I will," I promised, snuffling quickly.

"I don't want to go," she said, stooping to slide into the car.

"I'll call you Sunday night after the water board meeting," I promised.

"Oh, good. I wish I could be there to see Al Parry's face."

"I wish you could, too. But now, you'd better go," I advised. "You never know how long it will take to get through Seattle."

She blew her nose, then shifted into reverse and pulled out. I watched until I could no longer see the car.

I felt dispirited for the next two days, went about my duties with no enthusiasm. More leaves were beginning to fall.

The dry summer made them give up their precarious hold sooner, but nevertheless, autumn was almost upon us. I suspect everyone my age feels mildly depressed at the end of summer. There is no logical reason to equate the seasons with living, but we do. I am well into the autumn of my life, but I don't like to be reminded of that fact.

Of course, Jake's warnings made me much more aware of my inevitable mortality. Dying was not something I was ready to do. As I told him, I'd be careful, but I certainly had to admit that only Cyrus's intervention had saved me from the poisoned cookies. It was impossible to guard against everything, and dwelling on the possibility did no good whatsoever. I determinedly put the subject out of my mind.

By Sunday, I began to perk up. The water board gathering was probably the first one I'd anticipated with something approaching pleasure. Cyrus offered to drive. The meeting was scheduled for one o'clock and then everyone was to share a potluck. So we both had offerings to carry. It was my first ride in his little red toy.

"Why did you buy such an impractical car?" I asked as I stowed my carefully packed rice, artichoke and chicken casserole in the diminutive trunk.

"Why not?" he asked. "Why be stodgy? Why not have fun? I'll show you."

Before I realized what was happening, we'd detoured, and were soon sweeping around corners on the Pipeline, a road that climbs precipitously behind town. I hung on. "Cyrus," I began after I gulped at one particularly tight corner, "aren't you worried that . . ."

"Worried?" he interrupted. "Whatever for? I'm a perfectly capable driver," he said. "Always wished I'd gone into the Air Force instead."

"Well, you're not flying now. Slow down."

H grinned slyly. "Come on, Donna. Don't be stuffy. Relax."

To my surprise, I found that I was able to. As we swooped down a dip, I remembered how much I'd enjoyed roller coasters when I was a kid. I actually was disappointed when he said, "Guess we'd better turn here. This is one meeting we don't want to miss, right?"

"Right," I agreed. As we pulled into the Lutheran Church parking lot, I said, "Cyrus, that was really . . . really quite exhilarating."

He looked very happy. "Next time, Donna Rose," he promised, "I'll let you drive."

As I walked to the open door of the hall, I was picturing myself behind the wheel of the red car, until reality intruded. I looked around the hall. Same people I always saw at meetings wherever they were held, except for more men in attendance. Didn't matter what group, they'd practically become interchangeable. Regardless of whether it was the Historical Society, the Friends of the Library, the Animal Protection group, I could count on seeing the same faces. I suddenly felt smothered.

I shook my head, trying to clear it. What was the matter with me? I'd always appreciated the comfort of being surrounded by the familiar. I don't really like crowds of strangers; that was one reason I never liked visiting Roberta in New York, I realized suddenly.

Maybe instead of the smooth plain of the familiar, I'd dropped into the uncomfortable abyss of a deep rut. Perhaps I should, after all, have joined Alice on her European jaunt. Or, perhaps all I needed was a change of some sort here.

"Don't you want to go in?" Cyrus's voice intruded on my thoughts.

"Of course. What makes you think I don't?"

"Because you don't usually hesitate for five minutes with one foot over the threshold."

"Oh, come on. It hasn't been five minutes." I placed my foot firmly inside. It had, indubitably, been hanging in suspension.

Two of the Lutheran women who organized these things as fund-raisers relieved us of our food, and I stood there, indecisively. For once, I didn't feel like socializing. Cyrus was snared immediately by a covey of widows. Why is it that some women feel such a lack in their lives when they no longer have a mate? I remembered the husbands of two. Both had become querulous, shriveled old men without a new thought in their brains. Surely their absence was not cause for a frantic search for a replacement?

Cyrus, no doubt, was basking in the attention but, to my surprise, he caught my eye and waggled his eyebrows in a clear message of, "Get me out of here!" I leaned back, smiling smugly.

But then I remembered a time or two recently when *he* had rescued *me,* and I relented. I sidled into the group of women who would have reminded me of sparrows had their plumage been more subdued. "Cyrus," I said, taking his arm, "didn't you promise to help set up?"

"Oh. Oh, yes," he said. "Excuse me, ladies. I was so engrossed I neglected my duties."

They chirped their responses and we edged our way toward the kitchen. "Did I?" he asked.

"Not that I know of, but I thought you were signaling that you needed rescuing."

"Indeed. There are a number of intelligent, interesting women in Cedar Harbor, but not in that group."

Who? I speculated. "We'd better at least make a pretense

of helping." I pushed through the swinging doors to the kitchen area.

I knew most of the women. Noreen Parry was leaning over the oven, rearranging casseroles so she could squeeze one more in. Poor Noreen. It's sad that wives so often must suffer from the misdeeds of their husbands, and this afternoon's affairs were likely to be as distressing to her as to Al.

Gloria Larson hovered over the cakes and pies, talking to herself. "Too many desserts," she muttered. "I knew we should have planned this instead of letting chance take care of it."

Carrie shot a mutinous glance in her direction, then saw Cyrus and me. "Hi, there," she said. "Oh, Cyrus, just what I need. Manpower. Can I prevail upon you to help me move the tables in the other room?"

"Delighted," Cyrus said cheerfully. "Where do you want them?" They disappeared through the swinging doors before I had a chance to speak to Carrie. It was just as well. I wouldn't want to discuss the possibility of her working at the hardware store in front of others. I'd talk to her later, after the meeting.

I glanced at the desserts Gloria had been arranging. Didn't look like too many to me. Naomi's rum cake always was eaten in nothing flat, and that chocolate cake would be, too. There was a layered fruit thing that looked scrumptious, and a plate of fudge brownies. I'd be surprised if there were more than a smidgen left of any of them by the time we were done.

I went back into the main room. Al had arrived, and was fussing over papers with Kirk Bentner at the table where the board would gather. I glanced at my watch. Five to one. Cyrus and I had almost dallied too long.

As I had expected, the crowd was not large. Too bad. We

should have spread the word that the meeting would be more interesting than usual. People began to drift toward the chairs, and the board to the table. Finally, Al pounded the gavel. "Will the meeting please come to order?"

He didn't know, I thought, that he had just pounded the nails in his own coffin, the one where all his ambitions and greedy manipulations were to be buried. I leaned back in delicious anticipation.

CHAPTER XXIII

"I'm happy to report," Al began, "that we have the water system in tip-top shape. The board has been diligent."

Oh, the phony. As if we'd had anything to do with it. Kirk Bentner was the one responsible. Lyle, if I recalled correctly, had made the fortuitous find of the young man shortly before I joined the board. Kirk had taken a real interest, unlike some of his predecessors, and come up with some innovative suggestions for improving the system.

"I'm going to begin by asking Kirk to give us an overview of what we've accomplished."

Kirk began by saying, "Our supply is holding up nicely, thanks in large part to the cooperation of everyone in following our schedule and conserving water during these dry months." Beside me, I sensed Cyrus stirring. I ignored him. Kirk, possibly, was avoiding glancing in my direction. Well, let them fuss. I did my part as much as anyone in cutting back on water usage. I just did it in different ways.

The maintenance manager spoke for only ten or twelve minutes, but even so, I saw several in the audience glance at their watches. The potluck and socializing were what some of them were here for. That, plus being sure that we didn't increase rates behind their backs.

I wondered when Cyrus planned to drop his little bombshell. He leaned back in his chair, smiling slightly, as if he had nothing on his mind. Well, it was his find and his to handle.

Still, I, too, became impatient as the meeting droned on. There's always someone who wants to object to plans, usually some elderly man who was in on the construction of the original system and feels that he knows more about it than anyone else. This time, there was a business-type woman dressed inappropriately in a suit, who held a calculator in her hand as she questioned some of the figures.

Eventually I grew impatient and whispered to Cyrus, "When are you . . ."

"Shush!" he interrupted.

Finally Al got to the last item on the agenda. "Well, it's time to elect the new members of the board. Will Susan Reilly and Will Corrigan please stand? These fine people have volunteered to fill the two vacancies on the board." They both rose reluctantly, looking embarrassed, and sat down quickly.

Then Cyrus made his move. "Al," he said, holding out a hand, "may I say something?"

Al looked irritated, but conceded, "Of course. The floor is yours."

Cyrus stood. "I've checked the bylaws and don't find anything concerning conflict of interest. However, I think the community would agree that our board members should not represent a faction that might come into direct conflict with the board, am I not right?" A murmur of interest rippled through the audience. Susan glanced at me nervously. Oh, dear. She probably thought I'd stirred up trouble and he was referring to her.

"Get to the point," Al said crisply.

"I will, Al, I will. The point concerns you. Is it not correct that you have recently become a major shareholder in Gasper Enterprises?"

The hue Al turned put to shame any of Chief Donniker's

222

peculiar colors of frustration. Al, to put it succinctly, resembled a plum. I glanced quickly to the back of the hall. Hadn't I seen that new young doctor, Stan Chung? Yes. Good, he was here in case he was needed. I sincerely hoped not.

Al sat immobile, apparently unable to speak.

"I have papers here that prove . . ." Cyrus held out a brown envelope.

"You don't need to." Al's head sank to his chest.

Michael was the one to speak through the hubbub that developed in the audience. "Al, is this true?"

He nodded.

"In that case, I think Cyrus is right. I'd suggest you resign right now and let us choose someone else. You know the question of the Shadybrook Meadows permits is highly controversial."

Al pushed himself to his feet. "I resign." He picked up the papers in front of him and stumbled away. Noreen, her eyes wide, met him and took his arm. As the audience grew silent, they left through the front door.

Why was it that I didn't feel a sense of triumph? Al had suddenly become a sad man. A sad, rich man, I reminded myself.

Michael, to my relief, took charge. "We need a volunteer to replace Al on the board," he said.

After a period of silence, with everyone avoiding catching Michael's eye, Stan Chung spoke up. "I'll do it, if you want me."

Good. I'd been impressed by him. He was typical of many of the board members in the past, a newcomer who was not yet aware of the frustrations of belonging.

We went through the routine of getting him, and the others, elected, and then Michael spoke again. "We'll need a new president, of course. I'd like to nominate Cyrus Bates."

"Hear, hear," someone in the audience said, and everyone laughed.

Cyrus's mouth dropped open, then shut with a snap. He was trapped. There wasn't anyone else logical. Even with women's lib, they would never have chosen me. And the other three were all newcomers. Poor Cyrus. "I second the motion," I said, smiling at him.

The food had been delicious, as always. I let one of the churchwomen relieve me of my plate. I'd been lucky enough to snare one of the pieces of rum cake before they all disappeared. Cyrus, seated beside me on a folding metal chair, was slowly dissecting a large slab of chocolate cake and trying to juggle a cup of coffee at the same time.

I sighed. "It wasn't as much fun as I expected."

He nodded agreement as he swallowed some coffee.

"I suppose it never is . . . retribution, I mean."

He shook his head.

"Don't you have anything to say on the subject?"

"I'd have more to say if I weren't concentrating on trying to eat this cake from a confounded paper plate with a useless plastic fork," he said.

"Well, next year, when you're president, you can suggest we spend more money on better utensils."

"You didn't have to second the motion." He took another bite of cake.

"Oh, come on. Somebody had to do it. It was a foregone conclusion, after all."

"If I'd thought of it, I'd have nominated you."

Just then I noticed Gloria, obvious in her brilliant purple dress, weaving through the chairs toward us. She looked purposeful. Oh, Lord, what did she want? I should be feeling sorry for her, too, I knew, what with the wounds of Mary's suicide reopened. She was a difficult woman to feel much sympathy for, though. Still, I kept my expression somber as I raised my eyes questioningly.

"I noticed you don't have any dessert," she said, holding out a plate she was carrying, "and we *are* getting low. Thought maybe you'd like to try this carrot cake someone brought at the last minute."

"How kind," I said. "But I've already had dessert. Couldn't eat another bite."

Cyrus leaned forward, his eyes covetous. "Carrot cake? I do believe I . . ."

"No, you don't," she said, laughing and pulling the plate away from his reaching hand. At least her mouth was laughing, but I didn't think her eyes were. But then, a real sense of humor was notably lacking in Gloria's makeup. "You haven't finished what you have. We don't want you getting plump, now, do we?"

He glanced down at his taut stomach.

"Besides, we're running low on desserts. I'll just find someone else." She turned her back and again began making her way through the crowd—straight back to the kitchen.

I stared after her. "Cyrus, are you thinking what I'm thinking? That didn't make one bit of sense."

"You're right." He glanced around rapidly, searching for a place to divest himself of plate and cup.

"I'll go," I said, springing to my feet "and be sure she doesn't dump that in the garbage. I'll make some excuse. You find Jake, just in case?" Without glancing back to see if he was following orders, I tore for the kitchen.

"Excuse me . . . pardon me . . ." Why was it that the crowd seemed to have closed around me? "Well, hi, Marge, haven't seen you in a long time. I wish I could talk now." I excused myself much too abruptly from a woman whom ordinarily I'd have enjoyed speaking with. "Sorry . . ." I'd stepped on someone's toe.

I pushed through the swinging door into the kitchen. Several women were working there, but no Gloria. Then I spotted her.

In the alcove that led to the back entrance, the one that went outside, Gloria fumbled with the door handle. She was having difficulty because, in her hand, she carried a cake pan. One that, even from where I stood, I could see was full of cake.

"Gloria," I called.

She shot me one frantic glance, then slid through the door and was gone.

CHAPTER XXIV

Gloria! Why Gloria?

My brain whirled as I dashed through the door, trying to concentrate on catching up with her at the same time as I tried to reason out why she hated me so. I paused for an instant, scanning the parking lot. People were beginning to leave the meeting, so cars were backing and maneuvering past strolling walkers. Was she in one of those cars?

No, wait. Did Gloria drive at all? Did she even own a car? I didn't remember her ever arriving at a meeting except by walking or having hitched a ride with someone. Her house was only two blocks away. Was that where she was headed?

A flash of purple across the lot caught my eye. She was there, dodging past a van. She must have hidden behind it for a moment. I took a deep breath and then charged in pursuit.

People stared open-mouthed. It's not usual to see a woman of my age accelerating at the rate I was doing, especially a woman who foolishly had chosen to wear a straight skirt and blouse instead of her usual pants. My pantyhose didn't like the unaccustomed movement, either. I felt that pop and slither that indicates a large hole and run.

"Gloria! Wait!" I hollered. A foolish move. All it did was use some of the air I should have saved for breathing. She flashed a frantic glance over one shoulder, then disappeared around the large cedar that graces the corner of the church grounds.

Where was she headed? Not home. She ignored the side street that led toward her house, instead shot diagonally across the intersection toward the group of stores that tries to impress people by calling itself a shopping center. Still clutching the pan, she ducked down the alley behind Mason's, the supermarket.

I was gaining as she disappeared from view around the back corner of the store, so I skidded to a stop, confused. She'd disappeared. Where on earth could she have gone? I edged forward, sliding my feet as silently as I could. Thank heavens I'd worn a pair of rubber-soled flats instead of the moderate heels I'd considered.

A large truck blocked my view, so I hurried past. And there she was—at the big blue dumpster behind Mason's. She was struggling to raise the lid with one hand while clutching the cake pan in the other. As I rushed forward, she succeeded in raising the lid enough to slide the pan through. The lid shut with a reverberating clang.

Only then did she speak to me. "Why, Donna," she said breathing hard. A sickly smile spread across her face. "Whatever are you doing here?"

Did she really think that I hadn't figured out why she needed to get rid of that cake? "Why did you try to poison me?" I wheezed out of lungs that were gasping for air. We both panted for an instant, staring at each other. The fake smile disappeared, to be replaced by the most malevolent stare I'd ever had the misfortune to be the recipient of. Considering some sixth-graders' attempts, that was saying something. Her dark eyes bored into mine, and spit flew as she said, "I hate you."

"Why? Whatever did I do?"

She moved, her head thrust forward, and I backed away from all the evident malice. She took another step, and I backed even further. "You knew, didn't you." It wasn't a question.

"Knew?" I squeaked. "Knew what?"

"You knew that that despicable man abused my daughter. He put his filthy hands all over her body, then he raped her, and you didn't do anything. She killed herself, and you didn't stop her."

"What? What ma . . ." I must have been dense. "Oh. Lyle Corrigan." Was it *child* pornography he had in his collection that Will destroyed? It must have been. Why ever didn't Will tell us? I thought. Maybe we could have figured this out. Mary . . . Jolene . . . Nausea swept over me at the thought, and bile rose in my throat.

"You knew." Again she pushed her face in mine and I stepped backwards.

"Of course I didn't know. I had no idea."

"Mary always confided in you. She told me she did."

It was true that I had begun to develop a rapport with the girl. It had been clear that she had no one at home she felt comfortable talking to. But then, what sixth-grade girl does?

"I had to wait until Jolene came back home to find out why my daughter hated life enough to end it. That man raped Jolene, too, and she'd been through therapy. Part of her cleansing was to tell me. Cleansing! Mary didn't have a chance for therapy or cleansing or anything else. Jolene knew what her father was like, and she invited Mary to spend the night anyway."

"And Jolene . . ." I swallowed hard, but the taste remained, "Jolene had to die because of that?"

She bobbed her head, hard. "She was going to run away. The police thought she had killed her father. I persuaded her . . . I persuaded her to go with me to the beach where

229

Mary died. To make me feel better, I told her. She never suspected."

"But *you* killed Lyle."

"Of course. I only wish I could have made him suffer more. Oh, he suffered for a few minutes that morning on the dock. I reminded him that he was certainly headed for hell. But how I wish I could have tortured him as I've been tortured all these years."

"But why Marie?"

"She knew, too. She had to. She lived with the man. And you . . ."

It was then that she raised her left hand and revealed the knife. I recognized it. It was part of the set that belonged on the rack at the hall at the Lutheran church. I realized, too, that she'd backed me into a corner, the dumpster on one side, the blank wall of the grocery store behind me.

"And you were going to figure out it was me and tell the police," she said, waving the knife. "You asked questions and you found bodies. You're going to die, too!" She lunged forward.

I'd been watching that knife, and concentrating, and as she moved, I grabbed her wrist, hard, with both hands. "Cyrus!" I screamed. "Jake!"

I twisted with a jerk, glad that the muscles in my arms had gained so much strength from gardening. But she was strong, too.

"Let go!" I screamed. "Help!" People weren't that far away; maybe if I yelled loud enough, someone would hear. "Anybody, help!" Her other hand reached for my hair and began to yank. I kicked her shin, still hanging on, literally for dear life, to the arm with the knife.

And then I remembered the maneuver I'd seen demonstrated in a self-protection workshop many years before. It

Donna Rose and the Slug War

was designed to be used against men, but surely . . . I drew my knee up and thrust it toward her abdomen.

With a "whuff," she drew back and her arm relaxed ever so slightly. I twisted once again, even harder, and she fell to the ground, the knife slipping from her grasp. I sat on her, pinning her shoulders to the asphalt with my two hands.

As I struggled to get enough air into my lungs, I heard pounding footsteps. I looked up to see Jake, gun drawn, with Cyrus, his face flushed and his hair actually in a state of disarray, at his heels.

I took a deep breath, and said, "What took you so long?"

CHAPTER XXV

The first rain of fall had soaked the ground and more was forecast. We'd made it through another dry summer and we were no longer restricted on watering. Lovely. Except, I no longer needed to water. Might later, though, if the usual Indian Summer blessed us with clear, warm days.

It was time to start digging some of the more vigorous perennials. I'd choose some of the nicest, perhaps the Moonbeam coreopsis and the goatsbeard, and take them to Sue. The grapevine assured me that she and Jake had been seen having dinner together at the Harbor Inn, so perhaps she'd be in a mood to forgive me.

The county still hasn't lifted the moratorium, so the board, so far, has been spared having to make a decision on Shadybrook Meadows. Sometimes I wish Mark would get disgusted and take his projects elsewhere, somewhere that doesn't have a water problem.

My gardening expertise was brought into play shortly after the episode in the alley. Jake asked me to accompany the police when they, with a search warrant, surveyed Gloria's garden. Chief Donniker was noticeably absent. I found what they were looking for—a large pot of monkshood, tucked behind Gloria's compost pile. The stake identifying the nursery where she had bought it was still in the pot. When the police went to the nursery, the clerk remembered selling the monkshood to Gloria. She, incredibly, had actually discussed the poisonous properties of the plant with the clerk.

I hadn't needed the grapevine to find out that Carrie and Will had come to an understanding. They both had called me, pleased.

"I'm so grateful," Carrie said. "Will is such a nice man, and I truly missed being in business. Thank Cyrus, too, for putting the finger on Al. It was all I could do to keep a straight face at the meeting." Carrie clearly had not felt the odd sympathy that I had, but then, I'd never been as directly affected by Al's machinations as she had.

I had a long talk, too, with Will. Oh, we discussed Carrie, of course, and he was completely satisfied with her work. More than satisfied. But we also discussed Lyle's collection.

"I should have admitted that it was child porn," he said. "But it was so disgusting. I guess Roberta told you about how I came to find it?"

"Yes. She did."

"I never dreamed what he was really doing. I knew he was rotten, but I'd have stayed and tried to protect Jolene if I'd had any idea of how rotten."

Now, as I pried a reluctant clump of iris out of the ground, I felt good with the world. Summer was over, and with it the whole sordid story that in reality spanned twenty-three years and not just the one season. Cedar Harbor was back to normal.

A peculiar noise made me turn, the sound of something hitting the leaves of the forsythia behind me. I dismissed it. But then again I heard it, a soft plunk this time, on the camellia. How strange.

I straightened and listened. Just then, something flew by right in front of me, landing in the dirt hole where I'd removed the iris. I leaned over and found—a large slug. I knew there hadn't been a slug there a moment ago. Another thud, another slug.

Purposefully, but making no sound, I slipped over to the fence between my yard and Cyrus's. I peered through the knothole.

He was there, kneeling, Donna Two beside him and watching intently. I couldn't quite see what he was up to. I grabbed a small bench, set it down next to the fence and raised myself up on it.

"Cyrus," I asked, peering over the top, "whatever are you doing?"

He lifted his head and smiled. "Oh, I've turned my hand to inventions," he said. "A catapult. Quite clever, don't you think?"

"A . . . slug . . . catapult?"

He nodded. "Appropriate, I'm sure you'll agree." He sighed. "Life was getting so boring again. We can't have that, can we, Donna Rose?"

About the Author

Norma Tadlock Johnson previously lived in three western states and Mexico, as well as summering in National Parks, before moving to Camano Island, WA, where she was active on a local water board. She now lives in Burlington, WA. Her hobbies include reading, gardening and swimming, especially any place warm enough to snorkel, and she volunteers as a tutor in English as a Second Language classes. Her previous books include romantic suspense, juvenile novels, and romances written jointly with her daughter, a well-known writer.